Ghosts in the Walls

Spooky stories
inspired by real
history

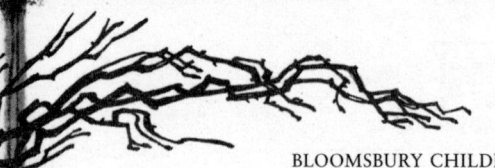

BLOOMSBURY CHILDREN'S BOOKS
Bloomsbury Publishing Plc
50 Bedford Square, London WC1B 3DP, UK
Bloomsbury Publishing Ireland Limited
29 Earlsfort Terrace, Dublin 2, D02 AY28, Ireland

BLOOMSBURY, BLOOMSBURY CHILDREN'S BOOKS
and the Diana logo are trademarks of Bloomsbury Publishing Plc

First published in Great Britain 2025 by Bloomsbury Publishing Plc

Produced under licence from Historic Royal Palaces Enterprises Limited, 2025
www.hrp.org.uk

Text copyright © Faridah Àbíké-Íyímídé, Alexia Casale, Joseph Coelho, Larry Hayes,
Jim Helmore Catherine Johnson, Sophie Kirtley, E.L. Norry, Jasmine Richards,
Imogen Russell Williams and Sam Sedgman, 2025
Foreword copyright © Yvette Fielding, 2025
Illustrations copyright © Pam Smy, 2025

The moral right of the contributing authors of this anthology to be identified as such
has been asserted in accordance with the Copyright, Designs and Patents Act, 1988

Pam Smy has asserted her right under the Copyright, Designs and Patents Act, 1988,
to be identified as Illustrator of this work

All rights reserved. No part of this publication may be: i) reproduced or transmitted
in any form, electronic or mechanical, including photocopying, recording or by
means of any information storage or retrieval system without prior permission in
writing from the publishers; or ii) used or reproduced in any way for the training,
development or operation of artificial intelligence (AI) technologies, including
generative AI technologies. The rights holders expressly reserve this publication from
the text and data mining exception as per Article 4(3) of the Digital Single Market
Directive (EU) 2019/790

A catalogue record for this book is available from the British Library

ISBN: HB: 978-1-5266-7119-6;
eBook: 978-1-5266-7384-8; Audio: 978-1-5266-7385-5

2 4 6 8 10 9 7 5 3 1

Printed and bound in Great Britain by Clays Ltd, Elcograf S.p.A

To find out more about our authors and books visit
www.bloomsbury.com and sign up for our newsletters
For product safety related questions contact productsafety@bloomsbury.com

HISTORIC ROYAL PALACES

Ghosts in the Walls

Faridah Àbíké-Íyímídé • Alexia Casale
Joseph Coelho • Larry Hayes • Jim Helmore
Catherine Johnson • Sophie Kirtley
E.L. Norry • Jasmine Richards
Imogen Russell Williams
Sam Sedgman

Foreword by Yvette Fielding

Afterword by Tracy Borman

Illustrated by Pam Smy

BLOOMSBURY
CHILDREN'S BOOKS
LONDON OXFORD NEW YORK NEW DELHI SYDNEY

CONTENTS

Foreword by Yvette Fielding   7

Click, Clack by Jim Helmore   15
THE TOWER OF LONDON

The Prince in the Painting by E.L. Norry   41
HAMPTON COURT PALACE

Charlie's Ghost by Imogen Russell Williams   61
KEW PALACE

The Haunted Masque by Faridah Àbíké-Íyímídé   85
BANQUETING HOUSE

Children of the Maze by Sam Sedgman   115
HAMPTON COURT PALACE

A Braid of Seeds by Joseph Coelho   139
KEW PALACE

The Sundial by Alexia Casale BANQUETING HOUSE	161
In this Still Place by Sophie Kirtley HILLSBOROUGH CASTLE AND GARDENS	187
Run, Rabbit, Run by Catherine Johnson THE TOWER OF LONDON	213
The Doll's House by Jasmine Richards KENSINGTON PALACE	235
The Executioner by Larry Hayes HAMPTON COURT PALACE	263
Afterword by Tracy Borman	283
Inspiration and Biographies	289

FOREWORD

I've spent many years investigating the paranormal and within that time, it's been an honour to have walked through every kind of building that's reputed to be haunted – from ancient palaces and castles, to old manor houses and even your everyday terrace house. In daylight, all these places seem so beautiful and fascinating in their own way. But as night-time falls, the structures become something different, and the haunting tales that you may have shrugged off earlier become a fearful reality.

To me, ghosts are very real – I've even been lucky enough to see one or two. I've also had the privilege of talking to a few of them as well.

Many years ago, I was given a private tour of

Hampton Court Palace. After I had been shown all the main palatial rooms and halls, I was to be taken up some backstairs known as the 'Silverstick Stairs'. I presumed we were heading off to some offices, but as we reached the top, my guide bumped into a colleague and they stopped for a moment to have a quick chat.

I froze – suddenly I was aware of a strange noise just behind me. It was soft moan. *A woman's moan.*

'Are you all right?' asked my guide.

I nodded and decided not to say anything. Even though she knew what I did for a living, I didn't want to scare the poor woman.

As we walked further down the corridor, I swore I could hear footsteps. I knew there was definitely a spirit following us.

'Has any ghostly activity been recorded in this area?' I asked carefully.

'Oh yes,' smiled the guide. 'This part of the palace is known for one particular ghost.' She nodded back towards the Silverstick Stairs.

'Oh, who's that?'

'Jane Seymour, of course.' She smiled again and moved her hands in a carefree manner.

I shuddered and rubbed my arms. The goose bumps had arrived and I suddenly felt ice-cold.

I looked over my shoulder, nervous and yet

intrigued to see if anything was there. Perhaps the outline of a person in an old-fashioned dress? But sadly, there was nothing. As I walked on, I asked myself, *Have I just heard Jane Seymour's ghost moan?* I shivered again. I was sure I had.

On another occasion, when visiting the Tower of London, I was in awe. What a place! Every inch of stonework, each door, gate and floorboard had a story to tell. If the walls of this place could speak, can you imagine what they would say? I walked across the moat and was delighted to be greeted by a very smart Yeoman Warder – I even did the touristy thing and had a picture taken with him! The Sun was shining and all felt great, but as soon as I walked into the main part of the Tower, that all changed.

A sense of foreboding crept over me – the whole place seemed to have taken on a darker energy. It had somehow come alive; black fingers of dread crawling towards me. I brushed off the creepy feeling and put it down to my imagination – we all know this place holds some very dark secrets and witnessed many a terrible death. I shook my head and told myself to 'get a grip'!

As I walked through the White Tower, where suits of armour are displayed, I suddenly stood stock-still as I could hear the extraordinary sounds of rapping and knocking thumping all around me. A sure sign of a spiritual presence.

I whispered quietly under my breath.

'How many of you are watching now?'

Well, the knocking fired back like a machine gun shooting rapid fire. Even as I moved out of that area, I could still hear the thumping echoing behind me.

It's safe to say, I believe that the Tower of London is absolutely teeming with ghosts – some good, and some very bad.

When tragedy, murder and sorrow occur in these places, somehow the energy of emotions are consumed within the very fabric of the walls and at some point someone is going to experience a replay of those actions along with awful, harrowing feelings. It can be terrifying, and at the same time very confusing. It can also be emotional, as when you see and feel something you cannot explain, your whole sense of being can be put into question.

As the great American poet Henry Wadsworth Longfellow once wrote, 'All houses wherein men have lived and died are haunted houses'. I think this is both wonderful and so true. If a location is haunted by a ghost, or by history itself, you're bound to sense or see something.

As you read the stories in this truly magnificent book, imagine yourself in each palace and try to envisage what you would do when faced with some kind of paranormal activity. Remember the stories, keep them locked in your brain and next time you visit a beautiful palace or castle, you never know, you may just come face to face with one of its long-lost occupants.

So, sit back, read on and later, when you put the book down, do try to … sleep tight!

Yvette Fielding

The Tower
Of London

CLICK, CLACK

By Jim Helmore

I didn't know her name back then. She would sit on a bench at the Tower of London and feed the birds. So, to me, she was just the Birdwoman.

Whatever the weather, she'd be there, scattering crumbs for the hungry pigeons and sparrows.

'Nice bit of grub!' she'd call. 'Come and get it!'

I saw her first on a cold day in February, tucked away by a wall towards the back of the grounds.

The birds seemed very at ease with her. Two of the Tower's ravens were strutting around by her feet.

And then I noticed something odd. Despite the freezing cold, she wasn't wearing shoes or socks.

I walked quickly past her, my thoughts turning to something else.

But on my next visit the following week, there she was again, in exactly the same place, as if she'd never left.

My grandad was one of the Yeoman Warders who lived and worked at the Tower. Perhaps he'd know who she was, I thought.

When I found him, however, Grandad looked baffled. He'd never seen or heard of her at all.

Grandad was a lovely man and I still miss him. I was 12 when all this happened – it's hard to believe that now I'm almost as old as he was then.

Most Sundays, I'd visit him at the Tower. He'd give a little wink when I arrived and wave me through the gate.

I'd get a delicious thrill from walking past the waiting visitors, especially on sunny days when the queues were long.

Most people who worked there knew me by sight, and I was able to explore every inch of the place.

As soon as I stepped inside, the weight of history pressed in around me.

It felt as though, at any moment, I might see a Tudor prisoner trying to escape or be knocked over by a hurrying footman with urgent orders from the King.

On each visit, I'd circle around the different parts of the site, soaking up the atmosphere.

The White Tower, with its four famous turrets, sits in the centre of a series of courtyards and towers built into two outer walls.

The Birdwoman's bench was near the Flint Tower, in the north part of one of these walls.

I saw her on each of my visits that spring, always wearing the same shabby dress and always with birds for company.

Then, one day in early summer, I was surprised to see a raven actually sitting on her shoulder.

As I came closer, the bird turned and looked directly at me.

'She's a beauty, isn't she?' the Birdwoman said. Her voice was a little husky, as though she hadn't spoken for a while.

I stopped in my tracks. She was facing the Flint Tower, with her back to me. There was no way she could have seen my approach.

When I didn't speak, the Birdwoman looked over her shoulder.

'I knew it was you,' she said, smiling.

Her brown eyes were faded and there was a smudge of mud on her cheek.

'You can feed her if you like,' she added, reaching into the pocket of her crumpled dress. 'She's always hungry.'

I was shocked when she reached over and dropped a large worm into my outstretched palm. The worm wriggled a little, cold and slimy.

Instinctively, I dropped it and immediately the raven hopped over, picked the worm up, then headed back to the bench and settled itself on the seat to enjoy its meal.

'Told you!' the Birdwoman said, laughing. 'Always hungry! And if you treat them right, always loyal.'

Her expression was suddenly serious.

'It's said that if the ravens ever leave the Tower, the Tower and England will fall.'

'Do you think that's true?' I asked, finally finding my voice.

The Birdwoman shrugged her shoulders. 'There are so many stories about this place, who knows?'

The raven stretched, shaking out its wings before hopping up on to the back of the bench. It stared first at me and then at the now-empty seat beside the Birdwoman.

'She wants you to sit down,' the Birdwoman said, smiling and patting the bench next to her. 'Let me tell you a tale about the Tower and you can decide yourself whether it's true or not.'

I hesitated, feeling a little uneasy, and had just decided to make an excuse about being late for something, when the Birdwoman interrupted my train of thought.

'You've got plenty of time today,' she said.

This was absolutely right. Grandad was busy helping another of the Yeoman Warders move, so I wouldn't see him until much later. How did the Birdwoman know this?

The raven was still staring at me too, its head tilted, almost daring me to refuse the offer.

And so, before I really knew what I was doing, I found myself sitting down.

'We won't keep you long, that's a promise,' the Birdwoman said, still smiling, and then she began.

***

This tale happened a long time ago, 300 years I should think, or thereabouts.

It concerns a boy and a girl who lived here then.

The boy's name was John. He was about your age, but taller and thinner. His face was always twisted into a frown.

John's parents died when he was young and many people tried to do him harm, but these beginnings gave him strength.

He clawed his way through life, grabbing every scrap of opportunity that came his way.

Eventually, after much hard work and a little good fortune, he found himself living here, at the Tower, as a servant.

On John's first day, one of the ravens hopped on to the path ahead of him and looked him over.

Ravens are always curious. They like to know what's happening, who's coming, who's going. But to John, the bird was purposefully standing in his way.

'Shoo!' he called. The bird stood its ground, fixing him with its beady eyes.

Like a lot of people, John believed that ravens were bad luck. And this big one, with its great beak, well, it must have been up to no good.

'Move it!' he muttered, aiming a kick at the bird.

The raven hopped away crossly and gave a loud cry. Ravens will soon tell you when they're not happy!

* * *

The Birdwoman let out a little chuckle and tickled the raven behind her, before continuing.

* * *

John and the birds were off to a bad start, and it didn't get any better.

The weeks passed and he began to settle into his busy new life at the Tower, cleaning and darning, fetching and carrying.

Though he avoided the ravens as much as he could, they were always there. If he didn't see them, he could hear them, calling to one other.

Then, one day, as John was coming past the Salt Tower, a raven flew from the wall and did its business right on his head!

His hair was always a mess, but now it was even messier.

Well, of course, John was furious! He threw a stone at the bird and missed.

AKK! AKK! AKK! the raven laughed down at him.

John's opinion of these birds was now set in stone and from that day on he became obsessed with the idea that they were deliberately out to cause him trouble.

For every little thing that went wrong – a trip on the stair, something important he couldn't find or job he forgot to do – there was always a raven nearby to blame, taunting him with its piercing stare.

He was constantly on the lookout for them, convinced that, whenever one approached, it was trying to provoke him, and he'd scowl or shout at it, angrily waving the bird away.

By now, all the ravens knew John, too. They remembered his cruel behaviour. They remembered *everything*.

***

Emphasising this last word, the Birdwoman paused for another moment, gave her raven another worm, and then carried on.

***

And that brings me to the girl in this story. Gwen, her name was.

It was because of John's fixation with the ravens, that he first noticed her. She was a few years older than him and worked in the kitchens.

Knowing the old superstition that the ravens must not leave the Tower, the cooks and their staff were encouraged to give the birds food.

This soon became Gwen's job. Every day, she'd take them out a bucket of scraps and the ravens grew to expect their treat.

If Gwen was late, they'd make impatient *tap-tapping* sounds and hop from one foot to the other outside the kitchen door.

Besides their usual squawking, ravens are excellent mimics. They can copy little sounds and bits of speech.

'Click, clack,' they'd say. 'Click, clack.' This was the sound of the door latch lifting.

'Creeaaak,' they'd call, just like the opening kitchen door.

Gwen would greet the ravens with a loud 'Good morning!' as she scattered their breakfast on the grass.

'Sleep well,' she'd whisper, before closing the door at night.

The ravens never learned to say, 'Good morning,' but they would sometimes repeat, 'Sleep well,' in a perfect imitation of Gwen's voice.

'Sleep well. Click, clack. Sleep well.'

Gwen grew to love the ravens and, as she treated them so nicely, the ravens came to love her, too.

They were her constant companions.

When there was no one else around, she'd talk to the birds – confiding in them her innermost thoughts.

She told them about her mother, who lived far away, and of her longing to return home.

Gwen was good to everyone else at the Tower, too – even to John, at first, giving him advice on difficult jobs that he'd be ordered to do.

John found this incredible. No one had ever shown him kindness before.

As the months went by, his thoughts would return more and more to Gwen, with her brown eyes and sad smile. He was more than a little in love.

As these new feelings for Gwen began to grow, so did his hatred of the ravens. For now, as well as distrusting them, he was jealous of them, too.

Why didn't Gwen look at him the way that she looked at them? Why didn't she tell him her secrets?

Perhaps, he reasoned, the ravens had some sort of strange power over her.

Then, as John was approaching the kitchens one evening, he overheard Gwen talking to the ravens about someone at the Tower. She was speaking in a tone he'd never heard her use before.

She didn't like this person. She couldn't bear the way he looked at her. He treated the ravens terribly …

Slowly, it dawned on John that she was talking about him.

Gwen's words cut like a knife. Embarrassment, then anger, began to pulse through him.

He cursed under his breath. He was furious with Gwen. Spiteful thoughts began to whirl in his mind.

There were stories about women like her, these treacherous thoughts insisted, women who formed unnatural bonds with animals. *Witches*, they were called.

Perhaps it wasn't the ravens who held Gwen in their sway, but Gwen who'd turned her sorcery on the ravens?

Witchcraft! That was it! And witchcraft would explain how he too had fallen so easily under her spell …

* * *

The Birdwoman was becoming agitated now, and she stopped to calm herself, looking around at the Tower walls, and then at me – almost to check that I was still listening – before taking a deep breath and speaking again.

* * *

And now we come to the final part of the tale.

An icy wind began to blow from the east. Winter had arrived at the Tower and within a few weeks, the great River Thames was frozen.

With the cold weather came a fever and soon poor Gwen was struck down.

Each day, the ravens would make *tap-tapping* sounds outside the kitchen door.

'Click, clack', they'd call, impatiently. 'Click, clack.'

But, when the door opened, a new girl brought them breakfast.

She tried her best to copy Gwen, wishing the ravens 'Good morning' as cheerfully as she could, but the birds ignored her. They danced about angrily instead and picked at their food.

John delighted in seeing the ravens so rattled.

Burying his true feelings for Gwen as deeply as he could, he pretended not to worry about her.

And, now that other people had started to recover from the fever, he convinced himself that she would, too. Gwen, however, grew steadily worse.

Though there were some with knowledge of medicine in the Tower, nothing anyone suggested seemed to help her.

Gwen was well-liked by everyone. Her closeness to the ravens was respected, too. With them in her care, they would surely never leave.

Eventually, one of the servants was ordered to fetch a doctor who lived outside the Tower. And that servant was John.

Suspicious of him, the ravens lined up on top of the wall and watched John leave.

'Click, clack,' they called. 'Click, clack.'

And when he was almost out of sight, one of them glided down to the road and began to follow him.

John's progress was slow on the frozen streets, but he hurried along as best he could.

In time with his footsteps, Gwen's overheard words repeated and repeated in his head. She didn't like him. She couldn't stand the way he looked at her.

Gwen's words were soon joined by John's own hateful thoughts.

She didn't need a doctor. She should use her own unnatural magic as medicine. She was choosing not to get better for the attention it brought her.

John ranted on to himself like this, until he reached a turning into a quiet side street where the doctor lived.

A large patch of ice covered the cobbles here and, too wrapped up in his own anger, he took his eye off the road, slipped and fell, badly bruising his knee.

It took him a moment to get over the shock of the fall, but when eventually he pulled himself up, in the cracked surface of the ice, John saw the reflection of a raven.

Turning to confront it, he found the bird standing on the window ledge of a house behind.

It was the same raven that had crossed his path on his first day at the Tower.

Unable to control his fury, John picked up a chunk of ice and hurled it at the bird with all his might. Once again, the raven flew off just in time, and the ice exploded against the window, smashing the pane of glass.

There were shouts from further up the street.

Furious, John hobbled off before anyone saw him, but this was the last straw.

It was the raven's fault that he'd fallen, he told himself, and surely it was Gwen's fault that the raven had followed him, too.

The ravens were her eyes and her ears. The spies of a witch! She didn't need anyone's help, and she certainly wasn't getting his.

So, instead of finding the doctor, he settled

himself into a nearby tavern and stayed there for an hour or so, wallowing in his own self-pity.

When John arrived back at the Tower that evening, a sombre mood hung over the place.

Mumbling excuses about not being able to find the doctor, he was interrupted and told the terrible news that Gwen had passed away minutes before.

Perhaps John's actions made no difference. Perhaps Gwen would have died with or without the doctor's help.

But John didn't believe that. The colour drained from his face.

Now there was a new feeling to add to the anger and the jealousy in his heart: guilt.

Gwen was no more. The only person that had shown him any sort of kindness had died, and it was all his fault.

**

As the Birdwoman finished her sentence, the raven on the bench behind us let out a loud cry. Another raven nearby joined in, and another and another.

AKK! AKK! AKK! they shrieked, their cries like the blows of an axe, echoing around the Tower walls.

I covered my ears at the ravens' terrible call, until abruptly, all was silent.

It took a moment for the Birdwoman to speak again.

***

That night, John couldn't sleep. He lay in bed with his eyes wide open. There was sweat on his brow, and guilt bubbled and squirmed in his heart.

***

Then, as the Birdwoman spoke, something started to happen to me. This is the part of my story that I find hardest to explain.

I could still hear her voice, but she and the bench and the birds began to fade away.

And, in the second it took me to blink, I was somewhere else entirely.

Day had become night and I was standing inside in a long dormitory, faintly lit by moonlight that spilled in through a series of small windows high in one of the walls.

I blinked over and over again, willing myself to wake up from this strange dream, but nothing happened.

There was a man lying before me in a rickety bed. I knew immediately that this was John.

One half of his face was shrouded in shadow, the other was a picture of fear in the pale light.

The Birdwoman's voice was just a whisper now. 'What have I done?' John asked himself.'

In front of me I could hear John's voice as he groaned, 'What have I done? What have I done?'

Tap-tap. Tap-tap. There was an unmistakable knocking sound coming from the dormitory door.

John looked across the room, and so did I. There was a pause. We waited, our ears straining to hear.

Click, clack. Click, clack. We heard the sound of the door latch lifting, though I could see quite clearly in the moonlight that the latch did not move.

Creeaaak! We heard the sound of the door opening, but the dormitory door remained absolutely shut.

John pulled the blanket over his head, moaning to himself.

Tap-tap. Tap-tap. The knocking on the door began again.

'Help!' I said aloud, afraid of who or what might be behind the door, but no sound came from my mouth.

'Help!' I called to the Birdwoman again, louder and louder until I was shouting. 'Get me out!

Get me out!' But my voice had vanished completely.

Click, clack. Click, clack. We heard the sound of the latch again, but this time, John threw the covers from his bed and jumped up.

Running to the door, he threw it open to reveal ... nothing but empty blackness.

Then, *AKK! AKK! AKK!* The cry of furious ravens erupted around us, filling the room.

Terrifyingly, there was no sign of the birds themselves! We could only hear their incessant, angry call.

And there were so many of them!

Horrified by the phantom birds, John raced out of the dormitory and I followed, hot on his heels.

We ran down a narrow stone corridor, up some steps, out of a door and on to the high open battlements of the Tower, our breath misting in the cold winter air.

AKK! AKK! AKK! screeched the ravens as they followed us along the stone parapets.

'Go away!' John pleaded.

This time, the ravens responded with their original chilling call.

'Click, clack. Click, clack.'

Glancing back over my shoulder, still I couldn't see any sign of the birds.

'Leave me alone!' John shouted, desperately.

Surely someone will hear him, I thought. *Someone will come*. But, apart from John's cries, all I could hear was the ravens.

'Click, clack. Click, clack.'

Though their cry wasn't loud, it was filled with more threat and more menace than the sound of any creature I had heard before.

I knew then that however hard John pleaded, the ravens would never leave him alone. They were here to take their revenge.

For a second, John's running became ragged, as though he had been hit by a hard object.

He stumbled, trying to find his footing, crashing into the outer battlement wall and collapsing to the ground.

I was about to help him up, when suddenly, the air was thick with flapping wings.

I could hear the sound of them rushing past me and I could feel the press of feathers against my head and neck, but still, I couldn't see them.

On and on it went. There must have been hundreds and hundreds of birds!

Very slowly, John staggered to his knees. His eyes were wide with absolute terror.

But it wasn't until he began to rise off the ground in an awkward, half-kneeling pose, that I realised he wasn't moving himself. He was being lifted up.

'Get off me!' he screamed, lashing out with his arms and legs. But his clothes and hair were held in the grip of invisible beaks and claws that wouldn't let him go.

Up and up John went, higher and higher, out over the battlements, until he was hanging almost upright, like a broken puppet, way above the oil-black Tower moat.

His body tensed, for what I assumed would be one final attempt at escape, but I've replayed that moment again and again in my mind, and I think by now he knew any further struggle was useless.

Instead, he roared out to his unseen captors, 'SHE WAS A WITCH! SHE DESERVED TO DIE!'

Perhaps I was just imagining it, as my mind tried to make sense of what was going on, but for a second, I thought I saw a teaming cloud of diabolical ravens swirling around him.

And then they were gone.

Abruptly, John began to fall.

I looked on in horror, realising that he wasn't dropping towards the moat at all, but to a spot just beyond, where the hard cobbled path ran away from the Tower.

He let out a long guttural scream as he fell, and I closed my eyes tight.

'Click, clack,' the ghostly ravens called. 'Click, clack.'

And then I heard the voice of the Birdwoman, though it was also the voice of Gwen, for I am sure that they were one and the same.

'Sleep well. Sleep well. Sleep well.'

All was silent.

When I opened my eyes, I was back on the bench by the Flint Tower and it was broad daylight once more.

I looked around, but there was no sign of the Birdwoman.

The raven on the bench gave me a final fleeting glance, then half-hopped, half-flapped away across the courtyard.

And, though I still visited my grandad at the Tower after that, I never saw her again.

***

I'm old now, but I've never forgotten what happened to me that day and I've never spoken about it to anyone, until now.

At first, I couldn't understand why the Birdwoman had appeared to me.

Then, as I grew up and thought more and more about her tale, it began to make sense.

I worked hard over the years until finally, I realised my goal.

For now I'm back at the Tower of London again, this time as a Yeoman Warder myself, just like my grandad.

I'm responsible for all the ravens that live here today, and I treat them very well.

'Click, clack,' they call when they're waiting for their breakfast.

'Click, clack,' they call, and I am never late.

'Click, clack.'

HAMPTON COURT PALACE

THE PRINCE IN THE PAINTING

By E.L. Norry

Hampton Court Palace
6 July – Schools Only Day

'Class, welcome to the Clore Learning Centre,' Mr Murphy says, as we walk through a red brick archway framed by gold leaves. Once the whole class is inside the light, airy space, he hands out clipboards and maps of Hampton Court Palace.

'The audio guide handsets will talk you through the history of the palace and help you complete your worksheets. Bluetooth headphones won't work with the guides, so if you need to borrow headphones, then line up here.'

I'm glad I've got my own wired earphones. Marley, my best mate, pulls some out from her blazer pocket too, and we grin at each other.

'Jay, wanna be partners?' she asks, untangling the wire and flicking biscuit crumbs off the foam coverings.

I nod. Marley loves history – ever since we did Egyptians in Year 3. If anyone can make today fun, it's her.

Mr Murphy claps his hands for silence.

'Complete your worksheet, then you'll have time to look around. Please remember that you represent the school, so be respectful. No running, pushing or eating. And keep your hands to yourself! We'll meet by the fountain at 1 p.m. The Warders in red coats are there to help, so if you need anything, ask one of them, OK? Check your map for your starting point and remember the focus today is the Tudors, specifically Henry VIII.'

Marley and I collect our audio guide handsets and loop our earphones around our necks. The class head up a long wide driveway. At the end is the palace entrance – a proper old-style castle with turrets of red brick and a flag flapping in the breeze. Walking through the archway takes us into Base Court, a big square with cobblestones and a fountain. This place is seriously impressive.

'Come on, this way!' Marley flaps the map in my face. She turns left and heads up some stone stairs.

'We're starting in the Great Hall. Then we end up in the Haunted Gallery.'

'*Haunted* Gallery?' I jog after her. 'It's really called that?'

'Cool, right?'

I pull a face. 'You don't believe in ghosts, do you?'

'Why not?' Marley shrugs. 'There's loads in life we can't explain.'

I tut. 'Yeah, the Big Bang, maybe, or why we dream.'

The Great Hall, with its high beams and huge ceiling, reminds me of a cathedral. I stare up at the wooden roof carvings and wonder how long it took to build. Mounted stag heads look down on massive, faded tapestries which line the walls.

'Those stag heads are way creepier than ghosts – they were real animals once. Ghosts are just things in stories made up to scare little kids.'

I go to plug my earphones into the audio guide handset, but Marley takes it out of my hand. 'You don't need the audio guide when you've got me,' she says. 'I know everything about the Tudors.'

I raise an eyebrow. 'Really?' Now's my chance to test her.

'Try me.'

I narrow my eyes and try to think of a question. 'OK. Who was John Blanke?'

Marley frowns. 'Who?'

'See!' I gloat. 'You don't know everything!'

Marley folds her arms and stares hard at me. 'You're suggesting you know something that I don't? About history?'

I take my audio handset back off her. 'John Blanke was a Black trumpeter who played in Henry's court.'

'If he was so important, how come I've never heard of him?'

I can't answer that, but I reply, 'He spoke up about getting better wages.'

'That is cool.' Marley looks impressed, but then her face falls. 'Oh no. Did I miss a page of the homework?'

I shake my head.

'No. I lost my worksheet, so I watched YouTube videos about Tudor public executions instead, and a video about him came on.'

The next room we enter has a curved stained-glass window full of bright blue and gold panes with Henry VIII's face in a circle in the centre. I get as close to it as I can – the colours are amazing. A warder dressed in red stares at us.

I point to the blue windowpane and Henry VIII's face. 'Someone liked being the centre of attention!'

Marley groans. 'Cross comedian off your future career list, won't you?'

I sigh. 'Just trying to keep this trip interesting.'

'It is interesting!' Marley says, desperately. 'You loved that play *Six* when we saw it.'

She was right, I did, and I didn't usually like musicals. 'Those were good songs.'

'Come on, let's go and see some ghosties!' Marley holds her arms out like a zombie and rolls her eyes back.

We turn into a dim corridor with lots of dark wood. The paintings there are three times my size, hanging on red and cream backdrops. We're the only people here and, even though it's sunny outside, the air here is chilly. The atmosphere feels heavy, as if a storm's about to come.

Marley's taking this way too seriously; she examines every painting and reads the information panels. With the Warders hovering there's no chance to mess about, so I may as well do some work. I glance at my worksheet and answer the questions about Henry VIII's wives. Something tickles the back of my neck and, wincing, I slap my hand on it.

'Better not be a spider,' I mutter, scuttling over to Marley.

At the end of the corridor are two lamps like giant candlestick holders, which cast dancing black shadows in between the paintings. The atmosphere feels murky.

'Why's it so dark in here?'

'To protect the tapestries. Sunlight would damage them,' Marley explains. 'What do you think life was like for them – the Tudors?'

I had no idea. 'Full of disease and rats?'

She whacks me playfully on the arm. 'At least try and appreciate this place. It's full of history. You can *feel* it.'

Marley is really into all this, but I can't see what we have in common with these dusty old kings and queens.

'They had no TV, phones or video games. Life must have been really boring.'

'Boring?' Marley exclaims. 'What about jousting and feasting and riding?'

I shrug. 'Still not as good as anything on the PlayStation.'

At the end of the corridor we turn right, and the backdrop becomes a dark rich green instead of red. The carpet under our feet is thick, and along the walls, framed by heavy velvet green curtains, hang various paintings in massive gold frames. They're roped off by twisted green and white ropes so that we don't get too close.

'This is the haunted bit.' Marley grins. 'Let's use the audio guides now, I want to hear more about the ghosts.'

The paintings dominate everything, and I shiver, suddenly cold. I whisper, 'These people in the paintings will be remembered forever … isn't that weird?'

'Yeah,' Marley replies thoughtfully. 'In some ways, they'll never die.'

A nervous giggle bubbles up inside me.

'Why are we whispering?'

'It just seems like we should … don't you sense it?'

'What?'

Her eyes widen. 'A presence. Think about everything that's happened here over the years. It's left a mark.'

I grin. 'You're off your head.'

'That was definitely true for two of Henry's wives!' Marley laughs loudly, and then quickly covers her mouth and whispers again. 'Catherine haunts this corridor. She was only 18 or 19 when she got beheaded.'

I puff air out of my cheeks in exasperation. 'Thought she outlived Henry?'

'That was Katherine Parr. It's Catherine Howard who's seen and heard running down this corridor, screaming. She thought that if she just reached Henry in the Chapel Royal then maybe he'd change his mind.' Marley sighs sadly. 'And we'll never know if he would have.'

'Ugh. Beheading by axe. Nasty way to go.'

Both of us fall silent. We put our earphones in and load up the audio guides. Pencils poised over the worksheets on our clipboards, Marley and I gaze up at the big painting in a gold frame of Edward VI.

The audio description tells us that Edward VI, the only son of Henry VIII and Jane Seymour, was crowned king at nine years old. But he died a few years later, aged just 15, on the 6th of July in 1553. We both pull one earphone out at the same time.

'It's the 6th of July today!' Marley says. 'Creepy … though not as creepy as his mum's heart being buried under the high altar here.'

She knew all the best facts.

'That's grim.' I crane my neck to look at Edward, so pale and serious. 'Happy death day, buddy.'

His eyes are dead and dark. His black and gold coat with huge, puffed sleeves make him look twice the size.

'His feet are massive!' I joke, but Marley's already put her earphone back in.

A bubbling hiss comes through my earphones, and I wiggle the jack back and forth to try and sort it out. That was the problem with these old style earphones – connection issues.

You're now walking through the Processional Gallery, following the footsteps—

There's a low buzz and then the recorded voice-over splutters out. A high-pitched whine shrills through my ears and I jerk backwards. I yank my earphones out. That hurt! I rub my ears and then examine my earphones – they better not be broken …

With one earphone dangling, Marley nudges me, reading from an information panel on the wall. 'Poor Eddie was 18 months old and already being compared to Henry. Bet he never got to do anything he wanted. Everyone was after his crown and bossing him around. His uncles completely betrayed him, you know.'

'But he was the King,' I reply. 'If anyone said no to him, he could just have them killed.'

Marley shakes her head. 'You don't really get it. He was still a child … even if he was called king, he never had any real power.'

'Kids being powerless … what's new?' I grumble, turning up the volume on the audio guide. I put my earphones back in. The crackling fades and a posh boy's voice says clearly and loudly:

My father's palace, crafted for a King's delight. Marvel at our opulent chambers and the life we led!

This is more like it! I step right up to the rope, staring at his picture. A king, and only three years older than me. The info panel says we share a birthday – 12 October. Now that *is* spooky.

The audio carries on: *I am Edward, departed from this earthly realm. At the age of nine, I was made a king. At 15, I was dead. A brief life indeed. Since then, I have lingered in death's embrace for five centuries, yet I do not crave eternal rest any longer. I yearn for the joys of jousting and archery, the merriment of feasting and the delights of entertainment and good company.*

The audio was brilliant! This is how you make history interesting. Where did they get such a good actor from? I turn to ask Marley, but she's wandered off down the corridor. I watch her scribble one note after another.

I can't stop staring at Edward's dark eyes. His expression is so serious. Marley is right. He should have had fun, not been expected to guide the country. That would suck – even if you were king.

Your gaze, fixed and full of wonder, meets mine own. Approach. Jay ... let your imagination soar.

Become a part of my father's grand Gallery. Feel the mantle's weight upon your shoulders, grasp the sword's hilt in your hand. Imagine the weight of being king. The power, the glory, the adoration.

What? Did I hear my name? The actor's now talking to me? How do they do that? I scan the corridors for hidden sensors. Maybe they pre-programmed the audio guides earlier, getting our names from when we signed in.

Help me! My uncles torment me in death as they did in life, with their manipulations and their demands. Thomas and Edward, always fighting, envying one another, and playing me as if I were a pawn. Thomas went from smuggling me pocket money to killing my beloved spaniel. Why must I endure their torments any longer?

As I turn back to the painting, a surge of heat rushes through me, like I've stepped out into bright sunshine. I'm anchored to the floor as though there's a magnet underground, stopping me from moving.

Please, I need an understanding ear to listen to what ails me ...

The bright flush of heat which felt like sunshine snaps off. Now it's like I'm inside a weighty, rolling storm-cloud and my eyelids droop, feeling heavy, like that moment just before sleep.

The painting: his eyes are deep and dark and steady.

An ocean of slick, black oil. My stomach twists and squeezes tight as I try to take my earphones out, but find my arms pinned rigid against my sides.

What's happening? I yell, but my lips don't move. They're tightly pressed together. My tongue is limp and useless, sitting in my mouth like a fat slug. The scream I need to shout out loud is only in my head. Thoughts explode like fireworks – *what's going on? Why can't I move?*

I can hear the faint scuff of Marley's shoes as she moves on down the corridor.

I try to turn my head to see her but can't. I try to scream, focus on opening my mouth or tensing my jaw but ... nothing. Not a squeak or puff of air. But I can feel the banging drum of my heart, stuttering and seizing.

Marley, come back! I try again. I'm paralysed ... but why and by what? How is this happening? How long will I be stuck here unable to move a muscle?

If Marley would come back, then maybe she could help. I want to blink ... my eyes feel so dry, but there's nothing except the rasping voice which keeps crackling in my ears.

Now you may feel as I do. Come yet closer. With that device in your hand, I know you see and hear me. Though it took years to comprehend the workings of such things, time has been my ally. We share so much, you and I.

My brain leaps and flails as I try to make connections. Am I moving ... swaying? I feel like I'm about to be sick. My stomach swirls and drops, as if I'm riding a rollercoaster.

I feel a prickle, an itch, as something trails down my cheeks. Are those tears?

Fear not, for setting me free renders a noble deed. I, Edward VI, shall now reside in a new form.

Reside? Doesn't that mean ... live in? Does he mean *me*?

Marley heads back my way, waving. Finally, finally! I see her out of the corner of my eye. She'll help me out of this ... whatever *this* is. But then a roaring *whoosh* thunders all around and I'm sucked into a swirling vortex where everything tips upside down, back to front, and rips inside out. A rushing waterfall pounds in my mind.

Darkness. No sound. No movement.

Is this ... death?

Then, as if a very long time has passed, everything has changed. I'm somehow looking down on Marley from a high angle. I'm no longer stood next to her, but ... someone is!

Marley's hand is on their arm, and she tugs their sleeve. A boy is next to her and he grins, rubbing his arms as if trying to warm up. He looks like me, but he isn't me.

I'm here, I try to scream. I can't feel anything any more, not even the banging of my own heart.

The boy in front of me – the one who has taken my place – stares up at me. He clears his throat. 'Thank you for your service.' Although he does a bizarre little bow, his eyes are blank and unsmiling.

Marley sighs. 'Enough paintings. I can't believe you've been here this long! I called for you twice,

The Prince in the Painting

but you looked like you were in a trance. Let's check out the kitchens, there's a whole room called the meat room.'

'Ah, yes. The scent of roasted pig is music to my ears. Long have I dreamed of the succulent juices dripping down my chin!'

'You're hilarious!' Marley's eyes sparkle.

Don't you know me, Marley? I want to cry out. *That's not me!*

The boy who isn't me, will never be me, but has stolen my life and my best friend, says, 'Don't fret, young maiden. I will be around for a long, long time.'

They walk away and their laughter echoes through the deserted corridor.

My mind swirls with darkness and frantic, silent screams rage. Panic smashes against my skull like birds beating their wings against glass.

That voice in my earphones wasn't the audio guide. Edward had somehow spoken directly into my mind. Somehow he'd switched places with me ... but how? What did we have in common? Nothing. Nothing! Except a birthday ...

Now I'm trapped here forever. The boy in the painting. And today is my death day.

KEW
PALACE

CHARLIE'S GHOST

By Imogen Russell Williams

'Get a move on, Charlotte! You'll be left behind in a moment!'

Mrs Windsor's forced-cheery voice stung Charlie like a jerked rein. Heat climbed from her toes towards her chin.

Left behind? She hadn't wanted to come at all. Some Christmas treat, sitting in a hot loud car with Dad, two spoilt six-year-olds and Mrs Windsor, soon to be Dad's new wife (yeah, all the jokes about marrying royalty. That was why they'd come to the *Royal* Botanic Gardens, Kew.) She didn't want to look at too-bright lights in the December drizzle, squinting through misted specs while the terrible twins screeched and demanded. She wanted to be with Grandad.

Kew was a Grandad place. Visiting the Botanic Gardens, and sometimes the Palace, had been one of their traditions. When he'd still been working as a landscape gardener, they'd come on the bus every month or so, but not at Christmas (they both thought the displays and stalls of the light trail were a distraction). Before he'd got ill, they'd been planning to build a tiny greenhouse together, a miniature Temperate House.

But now Grandad's memory was skipping, like a stone skimmed over water. He was struggling to take care of himself, forgetting to wash and change his clothes, and Dad and Mrs Windsor (Charlie couldn't think of her as 'Helen', let alone 'Mum') kept talking ominously in corners about safety and expense and residential care. The idea of Grandad somewhere not his cosy, ship-shape bungalow – with his garden and his fruit trees and his constant, tuneless whistle of concentration – was so hideous that Charlie's brain refused it. She shook it away like a wasp.

A gust of smoke from a brazier where people were toasting marshmallows stung her eyes as the twins started nagging for treats. 'We want marshmallows! And candy floss TOO-OO! You PROMISED!' As their chanting turned to a meaningless, maddening word-porridge, Charlie felt angry-hot despite the rain. She breathed deeply and stroked the frayed, soft cuff of her sweatshirt. *It doesn't matter if the twins are screaming. It doesn't matter that we're here. Can't hear them, can't see them. Really, I'm back at Grandad's, and the kettle's just about to whistle …* Another gust billowed from the brazier, pricking tears into her eyes.

'Come on, everyone!' said Mrs Windsor, even more cheery, hauling Aidan along as Dad scooped Tommy briskly on to his shoulders. 'This is supposed to be a treat! Try to smile, Charlie!'

A switch flipped inside. Being told to smile was Charlie's number one pet hate (she saw her dad's grimace as the words landed). Now she was no longer a person, but a slowly swelling ball of heat and fury. She had to get away before she exploded and took every last one of them down with her.

'Just got to …' She pointed beyond the fairy-light-draped food carts to the toilets. Before anyone could ask her to take the twins along too, she plunged out of the wet brightness, swerving quickly into shadow and the smell of green things asleep.

It was quiet under the sheltering trees. Grass and dropped leaves and needles cradled her feet, muffling her steps. Almost immediately, the calls behind her stopped. They gave up fast, didn't they?

Just like they'd given up on Grandad.

Branches stretched over the path, a looming shadow mass. The noise of the carousel and the 'wooo's from the light show cut out like they'd been swallowed. Charlie was going to sit quietly by the great greenhouse, just for a bit – but she was disorientated by the Christmas trail, and after a few minutes she realised she'd missed Temperate House altogether. Now she was deep in conifers, the smell of pine sharp in her chilled nose.

Those wretched kids. Charlie let the angry tears flood, scalding down her face, blurring her glasses. Shouting in her ears! Snooping in her precious stuff, breaking up her Lego! Bursting into her room, however big and red the 'KEEP OUT' signs she stuck to the door! They had six tantrums a minute and Dad just made endless excuses for them – 'they're only little', 'I remember you at this age, ha-ha! Ten times worse.' Well, she couldn't bear them. Couldn't bear the idea of them and their mother shouldering Grandad – and Charlie – out of her dad's thoughts. The trees' embrace felt comforting, though coldness was creeping under her collar and up her sleeves. A faint grey mist had gathered on the path.

And what would Christmas be like, if this was the 'treat'? This was the first year she would have to put up with the twins on the actual day. All her small, cherished rituals – cinnamon porridge with cream and grated apple, watching *The Snowman* and her old *The Wind in the Willows* DVD, blobbing just the right amount of cranberry sauce into its special glowing dish for the table – none of that would have the same quiet magic. And how would Grandad manage? She'd noticed he tended to stand and 'buffer' recently when there was a lot of confusing sound – and nothing was louder and more confusing than Tommy and Aidan turned up to sugar-max. But Dad was adamant about 'a family Christmas'. Well, those bellowing little beasts and their fake-smiling mum would never be Charlie's family.

Had the mist thickened? There was very little light – the sky was rain-cloud dank. Wiping her eyes, Charlie patted the back pocket where her phone sat sullenly, its ancient battery drained. No torch. She looked at the fog, now wreathing to knee-level. An optical illusion suggested it was giving off a faint light of its own – a sickly light that Charlie didn't really like. And she was getting colder. She'd better find her way to somewhere she knew.

As she walked, a sudden surge of anger fuelled her strides along the path. Let Dad have his new family! Let him have the twins, if they were so much better than Charlie. Get rid of her and they could have her room, rip down her soft green wallpaper and fruit-tree frieze, obliterate every last sign, like she'd never been there at all. Just like they wanted to do with Grandad. Tear down his bungalow and smother up the ruins.

Charlie checked herself. That last one – that hadn't been her thought. She looked down and jumped. The mist had risen in soft curds, piling to her waist. Worse, she could see the light wasn't an illusion – she could see her sweatshirt, colours drained in the cold, sick fluorescence. And, worst of all, she could hear the mist, or something inside it – coiling voices of rage and sadness and fear.

She took deep breaths, telling herself there was no threat. But her body knew better. Her heart clenched and stuttered, hammering at her ribs – then it stood still for a long, painful moment as she looked at the mist again.

Both ways along the path the grey waves came, stealing and creeping, plant-slow under the bowed branches. They billowed, slow and stealthy, changing tune with every twist: *that's right, Charlie, they don't want Grandad, don't want you – but we do. Come to us. Leave them to their noise, their selfishness. Let them have the screaming. We'll welcome you in our silence. Stay here with us. Be still.*

The waves exerted a soft pressure now, a sort of damp-duvet weight that climbed her body, slowing her down to a desperate, determined trudge, feeling its way up towards her face and throat. Instinctively, she knew she mustn't stop, she mustn't leave the path. If she stood still, she'd never move again – and if she followed the wheedling voices with their soft rage and entreaties, she'd wind up somewhere that was no longer a garden. Somewhere she was no longer Charlie Lindon. Somewhere she didn't exist at all.

The climbing pressure made it hard to breathe. Hard to think. Tearing herself loose with a huge, wrenching effort, she sped up to a trot, then a run, terrible wasp-buzz voices dive-bombing her ears. But the mist thinned out as she drove through it, and she felt a pang of hope, bound up with wild, painful wishing – *I don't want to be lost here and forgotten! Anything would be better than that ... even Christmas with the twins—*

Thud! Her toe caught agonisingly on a root midstride, breaking her momentum like the snap of a whip, and she slammed down on her palms, specs flying off her face. She patted about to find them before the mist came again to smother her up, perhaps forever, but her seeking hands met nothing but leaf-mould. Fear weighed down on her, pressing her deep

into the dirt of the path. She gave a dry little sob of despair as she crouched, paralysed by terror.

Then her trailing fingers brushed the cold metal of her specs. As she put them back on, she saw a small white bloom of light ahead of her, like the headlights of a tiny car.

Charlie's choking fear eased back, just a little. There was no mist gathered around the light. Scrambling to her feet, she headed quickly towards the glow as the grey continued to thin and she stroked her cuff for comfort. The path curved, the light-bloom widened, and Charlie saw a two-storey house with a thatched roof ahead of her, hunkered in a grassy fairy-tale clearing.

She knew where she was now. She'd been to Queen Charlotte's cottage before. It hadn't been open, but they'd sat on the grass outside, where

Grandad said there'd once been a menagerie, and had their picnic. (Grandad had strong ideas about picnics. Supermarket sandwiches and sausage rolls were strictly forbidden – you needed stinky cheese, thick-cut ham, baguettes, pickles, proper apples and jam tarts. And cloudy lemonade.)

The 'cottage' – really quite a big house, but toylike, like a giant's doll's house – was picked out in the cool white bloom of light, as if the sullen clouds had given way to moonlight. There were two doors on the ground level, bulky and braced with iron. As she pattered closer, the left-hand door eased open, spilling a warmer light on to the grass. Charlie pulled the door fully open and darted in, desperate to find refuge from the dangers in the trees.

It closed quietly behind her, making her jump. Should she have come in here? It felt safe – so much safer than outside. The soft pink of the little painted hallway had a velvety feel, like the heart of a flower. She peeked through into the room on her left, where the walls were painted a soaring blue under rows of framed pictures, and went in to see them close up, the same tiny figures repeated in different places and poses. She ran her fingertip along the smooth cool edge of one frame.

'That's my favourite, too,' said a voice with a faint accent.

Charlie whipped round. 'I'm sorry, I shouldn't—' Her apology cut off as she stumbled back, her heart hammering in her ears.

She knew it at once – this was not a living person.

Although the hovering image held the rough shape of a young woman, its outlines shimmered and rearranged themselves, throwing back uncanny light like a rippling, shallow pool. But the face was quite clear: a high forehead, large humorous eyes and a long neck. Charlie had seen that face in a portrait when Grandad told her about the cottage.

The figure wore a sharply corseted dress, surging out into a huge, hooped skirt. The watery gleam of silk and the little white fires spitting off diamond jewellery made its strange, shifting radiance more pronounced.

Charlie had escaped the horror on the path only to come face to face with a ghost queen – a woman who'd been dead for over 200 years.

'Welcome, child,' said Queen Charlotte, floating closer. 'Do not be afraid. You are safe here. Come, sit …'

She beckoned Charlie to an elegant, spindly-legged chair, and settled, glinting, in the one beside it. Charlie gingerly perched one butt cheek on the chair. She didn't know which was more terrifying – damaging an antique or talking to a ghost.

'What is your name, child?'

Charlie swallowed to unstick her throat. 'Charlie. That is – Charlotte. Your Majesty.'

'Ah! A fine name. One of the best,' said the sparkling ghost. She reached for Charlie's hand with her light-dappled fingers. It felt strange, but not unpleasant, like the warm bubbles in a foot spa. 'Tell me, Charlie. Why do you find yourself alone, in need of refuge?'

A memory of the fear under the trees washed over Charlie, enough to make her heart thud hard again. 'Um – something out there was chasing me. Do you know what it was? It looked like mist, but it felt ... like it wanted to eat me, or something.'

The Queen folded her hands, looking grim.

'I am not the only spirit who lives here, child. Any ancient house or home will have its ghosts, and these Royal Botanic Gardens are no exception. There is a botanist still labouring in the Herbarium who died over 140 years ago. Another Charlie, a devoted curator, remains loyal to the Temperate House. We are drawn to the work we did in life, and to the places we loved and do not wish to leave.

'But not all ghosts are gentle. In any great garden, any wood or maze or grove, the spirits of the place will gather. And in the winter dark, the malignant ones grow strong. They sense anger, sadness, bitterness, people burning themselves up like angry suns, and they crave to possess them.'

Queen Charlotte fixed Charlie with a kind but direct look.

'What anger and bitterness are you carrying then, child, to draw such spirits to you?'

Charlie sniffed back more tears. She couldn't remember the last time she'd been the focus of someone's attention, and the feeling warmed and calmed her. After a brief pause, she told Queen Charlotte everything: the twins' brain-melting tantrums, the loss of her tight little twosome with Dad and, most of all, Grandad – the person who understood her best. How he was struggling to be understood, his home and independence threatened.

When she finished her blurt, she felt embarrassed but relieved, like she'd been cured of a persistent headache.

'Poor child,' said the Queen softly, laying a soothing hand on Charlie's hair. 'Poor Charlie ... You know, my dear, when I came here from Germany, I was only 17 years old. Two hours after I landed, seasick and spinning, with hardly a

word of English, they dressed me up in a gown too big for me and off I went to be married to a man I had never even met. And my new mother-in-law! Ach, Charlie, she did not approve of me, even a little. Here – you can see it for yourself, as I am touching you.'

The blue wall wavered behind the ghost, and one of the oval-framed prints changed colour and began to move. Polishing her specs, Charlie saw Charlotte in the picture, very young and thin, wearing a heavy purple cloak and a dress crusted with diamonds, like a doughnut dipped in sugar. She spoke solemnly to a tall man in a white wig – the King? – who gave her a huge ring with what looked like a little painting set inside of it. Then Charlie saw an older woman with a high forehead and a narrow, measuring expression. She stared coldly at Charlotte, waving the attendants back to leave the new Queen standing alone. Charlie felt a stab of familiar, sympathetic loneliness.

'It was hard at first,' said the ghost. 'I missed my home, my forests. But I was a fast learner, and soon I found my husband and I shared a great love of these gardens – just as you and your grandfather do.'

The print faded, and a new one sparked softly into life. Charlotte was walking through a garden with a shallow basket on one arm, looking at leaves and blossoms with a focused care that reminded Charlie instantly of Grandad. The King was there too, not in his wedding finery but rough, comfortable clothes. Charlotte made an expansive gesture to the horizon, spilling flowers from her basket, and both of them laughed, looking at each other with great fondness.

The present Charlotte smiled. 'I always loved flowers. You know the bird of paradise flower was named for me? Such a fine, flamboyant, blue and orange fellow! However bleak the season, Charlie, there is comfort in a garden – caring for it or simply being in it. You know that. Hold on to the knowledge.'

She glided out of the room, making it clear without words that Charlie should follow. Charlie supposed you learned those things when you were a queen. She went obediently up the broad, shallow spiral of the staircase behind the shining ghost.

'My husband and I designed this place ourselves,' murmured Charlotte, her light pulsing shadows and warmth across the landing and the big, arched window. 'We made it our own. We needed somewhere that was not a palace; somewhere we could feel more ourselves. Perhaps you share that need, Charlie – perhaps you have such a place?'

Charlie's Ghost

At the Queen's words, Charlie felt the sleepy heat of Grandad's greenhouse, smelt the spicy tomato scent lingering in the wooden shelves and boxes. The sense of things contentedly growing was the purest antidote to school and its impossible demands. She'd found refuge in the greenhouse and potting shed since she could first toddle after Grandad, handing him stakes and seed packets and eating strawberries warm off the vine. Even the twins behaved themselves there, dropping seeds obediently into pots and trays and keeping their hands in their pockets.

At the top of the stairs, the ghost touched another door and led her into a sage-green room painted with an arching trellis of flowers, the curve of the ceiling echoing the swooping thatch above. Delicate chairs and settles stood grouped against the walls.

'Come in, and welcome, Charlie! This is my favourite room. We had picnics here, my dear King George and I, hidden away like children playing house. And later, how our own children loved it ... My Elizabeth the most.'

Charlotte moved towards something in the corner of the room, and Charlie briefly saw a second figure beside her: unmistakably Charlotte's daughter, her face serene and intent as her glimmering hand traced the lines of painted flowers on the walls around us.

The deep red of the nasturtium petals glowed beneath her touch.

'When she grew older, she painted these flowers to welcome her father back.' As Charlotte glided on to one of the settles, the sunny, hopeful light in the sage-green room clouded and dimmed like rain on a meadow. 'Do you know what happened to my poor King, Charlie? I imagine you must. People barely speak his name without adding "mad" or "madness" ...'

Charlie did know, but only vaguely – she'd once heard a teacher at school talking about old treatments for mental illness, and he'd mentioned 'Mad King George'. When she looked at Charlotte again, she saw the shining ghost was also growing dull, her hair fading, her shoulders slumped. She heard a new sound, too. A long way off, someone was talking, calling out something urgent – the words were muffled by distance, but the distress was as clear as a bell. Charlie hunched her shoulders against it. She recognised that distressed, frustrated tone.

'He was supposed to come for a tea party.' Charlotte smiled sadly. 'He had been getting better, you see. Elizabeth worked so hard on her design – and then the clouds opened and the King could not visit after all ...'

Impulsively, Charlie sat beside the fading Queen and took her hand. She felt the strange, bubbling warmth of her touch again – then a deluge of memories scoured her. She saw the King, flushed, shouting, shoving the smartly wigged staff. A dreadful glimpse of the King raising his hand, the Queen shrinking back. The King strapped into a chair, calling out hoarsely for Charlotte and his children, talking in low, forceful tones to people who weren't there. The King, weeping and wide-eyed, trapped in terrible silence. And Charlotte, crying in a stately bedroom as though she would never be happy again.

The Queen took her hand away gently. 'I prefer to remember him as my dear Farmer George, child. He was always himself, after all – even when his mind strayed far away into places of terror. And Elizabeth's work was not wasted, though her father didn't see it. She put love into something fine, and here it is, still, to give us joy. There are worse things to do in times of trouble. I think your grandfather would tell you that.'

Charlie swam up from the sadness of the memories, from her own huge, shapeless fear for the future, and remembered the little greenhouse she and Grandad had planned to build. There was an overgrown corner of Dad's skinny, awkward garden that was perfect, facing south-east. Confronted with Grandad's blueprint for 'a tiny plant palace' – and Charlie's unceasing enthusiasm – Dad had agreed to it, on the condition that Charlie did the donkey-work of clearing the plot.

But Grandad's memory had begun to glitch before they'd got started.

'I could still build my grandad's greenhouse,' she said slowly, her decision forming as she put it into words. 'He might be able to work on it with me – some of it, at least. He taught me how to put a timber frame together – just a cold frame, but still – and fit panels. And – I could try and teach the twins to help. They actually love growing things. And building stuff, when they're not screaming their heads off. That's why they're always in my Lego ...'

'That is a fine idea,' said the Queen. 'The hunters under the trees have no power over the open heart – the heart that embraces joy despite the sorrows that burden it. Come, Charlie, I have one more thing to show you.' She swept out of the sage-green room, her light increasing, wavering like water on the walls as she led Charlie down the back staircase. 'Oh, I had much joy here. There were animals like kangaroos roaming the grounds! Can you believe it? And I brought something from my first home here to share.'

In a small, soft-pink kitchen, there was a fireplace, stacked with apple logs that sprang into instant ghostly flame as the Queen touched them. Deep in the fire, Charlie saw an elegant room in which a young Charlotte pointed to a yew tree in a pot, its branches weighed down with riotous colour. Candles, bright baubles and little treasures everywhere: blank-faced baby dolls, thread-rigged sail-boats, clowns, balls, hoops, sweets in paper packets, red-polished apples, sticky glistening dates. Charlotte wasn't looking at the tree, though, but at the faces of the children clustered round it – transported with shock and delight, as if they were seeing real magic.

'Merry Christmas, Charlie,' said the Queen, as she let the fire fade. 'You have sorrow and challenges ahead of you, but you have the courage and tenacity to weather them, and I believe you have a great capacity for joy. Love your grandfather. Bring him leaves and seeds and blossoms and soil. You may find he remembers them when much else is forgotten.'

Charlotte touched the door that led back out into the gardens. 'My light will lead you back to the Palm House, where I think you will find your family again. You are not afraid?' She looked into Charlie's face and smiled, stroking back her tangled hair. 'Good. There is no need for fear, my resolute Charlotte. Only weather your sorrows and cherish your joys. Ah, yes – and build your greenhouse, however much the little boys get in your way. It will mean a great deal to them, too. What will you call it?'

'Charlotte's House,' said Charlie.

BANQUETING HOUSE

The Haunted Masque

By Faridah Àbíké-Íyímídé

Omari St Vincent never intended on breaking into Banqueting House. And yet here he was, standing right outside of the wide, majestic, stone-walled building at what felt like the dead of night (but was actually just around half past seven) ready do just that.

One might ask how Omari St Vincent, who had never broken a single rule, let alone broken into an actual building before, found himself in this position in the first place. What on earth might have possessed him to think that breaking into a historic royal palace was at all a good idea?

The answer to these questions will require turning the clock back to the events of exactly one hour ago to the start of it all.

And how did it start?

Well, it all started how most bad ideas start.

With a lie.

***

One hour before

The Whitehall City Drama Club were in the middle of rehearsals for their upcoming production of William Shakespeare's *Macbeth*.

Omari was sitting in a semicircle next to the other students who attended the club, holding a script in his hands as the drama club leader, Ms Kastril, stood in front of them all with an unimpressed expression on her face.

'This is unacceptable!' Ms Kastril said, her voice high-pitched and her face pinched. 'There are only two more weeks to go until the big production and most of you still haven't learned your lines.' Ms Kastril looked around the group.

'The only person who seems to actually be taking this play seriously is Edwina,' Ms Kastril said, gesturing to the girl seated in the middle of the room, who was smiling smugly at them all. Edwina was a know-it-all and made it her mission to make them all look bad. Omari fought the urge to scowl at her.

'One way that might help these lines to stick quickly is to familiarise yourselves with the setting,' Ms Kastril continued. 'It helps to learn some historical facts about the play itself to get into the minds of your characters more easily and set the scene.' Ms Kastril paused to grab a small stack of A4 sheets. 'I have prepared this worksheet for each of you with some interesting facts about the time period. For example, King James I, who many say the character Macbeth was inspired by.'

Omari took his sheet with an interest.

'Was King James a villain like Macbeth?' Sara, who was sitting next to Omari, asked.

'Probably to some ... but many would argue that his son King Charles I was the bigger villain. Interestingly, this community centre we're in is only a few minutes' walk from Banqueting House in Whitehall – which is rumoured to be haunted, but which is unfortunately currently shut for major renovations. Anyway, Banqueting House is where King James's son, Charles I was beheaded,' Ms Kastril said, with a small, scary smile.

'He was beheaded?' Thomas asked, his face shocked.

Ms Kastril nodded. 'Yes, for high treason. He took his power too far and too seriously. Many would call him a tyrannical dictator, just like Macbeth.'

Before she could continue, the alarm on her phone rang out, signalling the end of drama club, and group began gathering up their belongings.

'Well, I don't really need to do any more research. My mum took me to visit the real place that *Macbeth* is set ... in Scotland,' Omari heard Edwina say boastfully to the small group of drama kids.

'You went to the castle in Scotland?' Sara asked her.

Everyone looked impressed but Omari was not going to give Edwina the satisfaction. He kept his mouth in a straight line as he stuffed his script and worksheet into his bag and then shrugged his backpack on.

'What about you guys? What research have you done?' Edwina asked, her arms folded as she turned her nose up at everyone.

'I haven't really had the chance,' Pip said nervously.

'Me neither,' added Thomas. 'My mum's always too busy with work to take me anywhere.'

Omari was planning to avoid answering by making a swift exit from the hall, but before he could get to the door ...

'What about you, Omari? Done any research?' Omari could hear the mockery in Edwina's voice.

He hated how she thought she was so much better than everyone else.

'Actually,' Omari said, before he could stop himself. 'I have done some research.'

'You have?' Edwina replied, looking a little annoyed.

Omari nodded. 'Yeah, in fact ... I've done quite a bit.'

'Hmm ... where did you go?' she asked.

'I just ...' he began, trying not to look too closely at the expectant faces in front of him. The lie tumbled out of his mouth before he could stop it. 'Banqueting House. I went there and saw the place Charles I was beheaded and everything,' he said. He had technically passed Banqueting House one million times on his walk to and from the drama club each week.

Edwina looked at him with suspicion.

'But Ms Kastril said Banqueting House was closed for renovations, so how did you visit?'

Omari swallowed. 'I ...' he began, his voice shaking at the prickling feeling of Edwina's gaze

burrowing holes into his skull. 'I ... um ... snuck in,' he said, this new lie being conjured without permission from his brain. The other drama kids gasped at this revelation.

'How is that possible?' Edwina asked.

Omari shrugged, like it was no big deal. Everyone else seemed to believe him, their voices coming in a jumbled flurry as they asked him questions. He heard Thomas asking whether it was scary to visit, and Pip asking if there were really ghosts.

'Of course there were no ghosts,' Omari answered with a smile, relishing the annoyed look on Edwina's face at the attention he was getting. 'Or at least, I didn't see any.'

'So cool!' Sara said, looking impressed.

As they began to filter out of the hall, he felt someone grab his shoulder, their nails digging into him.

He turned to find the furious face of Edwina staring back at him.

'I don't like liars,' Edwina said.

'I'm not lying,' Omari replied with all the conviction he could.

She narrowed her eyes at him. 'Okay then, prove it.'

He raised an eyebrow, shouldering his backpack. 'Prove what, exactly?'

'That you snuck in. I dare you to sneak in again, tonight,' she said.

Omari's eyes widened.

'T-tonight?' he replied, barely masking his shaking voice.

'Yes, tonight,' Edwina said. 'And I want you to take me with you.'

***

And this is how he found himself outside Banqueting House with Edwina Park instead of being on his way home.

The two of them were looking up at the tall building, behind its iron gates, with a mixture of fear and awe. Omari had no idea how he'd got himself into this mess or how he would get himself out.

He felt Edwina's intense stare at the back of his head, her arms folded as she watched him.

'Go on then, show me how you got inside,' she said.

Omari swallowed, considering for a moment telling Edwina the truth, that he'd been lying before and he'd never snuck into Banqueting House. But then he thought about how she'd tell everyone and laugh at him and be even more insufferable.

He could do this.

This was just like acting. Even when you were nervous, you had to improvise and pretend you weren't.

'Well, first I have to open the door, obviously,' he said.

'And how are you going to do that?' she asked in a mocking tone.

He cleared his throat nervously, as a risky idea flittered into his mind. 'Well ... I know a thing or two about picking locks,' he lied, wondering how he was ever going to dig himself out of this. 'I won't be able to concentrate with you watching over me though, so you need to look away.'

Edwina rolled her eyes, but dutifully turned her back on Omari as he reached into his backpack uncertainly and grabbed the large paper clip from the worksheets Ms Kastril had given them, which he quickly began to unfurl.

He glanced around for onlookers and then he scanned the stone walls for any sign of a camera. There were none.

'Here goes nothing,' he muttered, as he approached the padlock on the gate. But before he even got the paper clip anywhere near it, he noticed, to his surprise, the gate was already unlocked – the padlock swinging open. Omari couldn't believe his luck! Maybe, just maybe, he wouldn't become the laughing stock of the drama group after all.

He stepped through the gate, looking back as Edwina turned towards him, clearly trying to hide her surprise. 'Told you I could do it,' he smiled. 'So, are you coming or what?' he asked, noticing now a strange expression on Edwina's face.

Fear. Edwina Park was scared.

She scowled at him and hesitantly followed him through the gate.

'You still have to open the main door,' she said in a low, disbelieving voice.

But she wasn't able to hide her shock when, after some surreptitious fiddling with the lock by Omari, the main door to Banqueting House opened, too.

This is a bit too easy, Omari thought to himself, feeling a little unsettled. But despite being afraid, Omari did not want to let Edwina win. So he took out his phone, raised the flashlight and took a confident step inside the dark beyond the door.

'See, nothing to be afraid of,' he said, although he felt his knees wobble a little as he peered out at the dark beyond that greeted them. 'Now you can see I did sneak in.'

He pointed his phone towards the unlit path ahead, and Edwina followed behind as he led them down a dark corridor. Beneath his feet, he could feel the unstable ground. He could hear the crinkling sound of his shoes against the plastic sheeting that covered the floor, protecting it from the renovations.

They walked straight for a few minutes and as Omari shone his light around, he could see a few signs.

One read 'DANGER AHEAD, PROTECTIVE CLOTHING MUST BE WORN' and next to it, another sign had arrows pointing up and the words BANQUETING HALL'.

'That's basically where Charles I was executed,' Edwina said. 'I think we should check it out, for research.'

Omari wasn't so sure about that, but yet again, he did not want Edwina to win this game of nerves and so he walked towards the staircase.

He was about to go up the stairs when suddenly he heard a low sound, followed by the crinkle of what sounded like footsteps on plastic.

He turned back sharply to find Edwina standing behind him.

'What?' she asked.

'Did you hear that?' he said.

'Hear what?'

He paused. 'Nothing, I guess,' he said, as he moved to go back up the stairs.

Maybe it was all in my head ... he told himself, even though he swore he heard the echo of a snicker.

They made their way upstairs, his heartbeat

slowly returning to its regular state.

The entrance to the Banqueting Hall was heralded by a set of heavy oak doors, which they pushed open before entering.

Much like the rest of the building, the Hall was covered in plastic sheeting. But despite being in a somewhat shabby state, with some of the floorboards up and the walls stripped back, exposing the old stone layering of the building, it was possibly the fanciest room Omari had ever seen. There were pillars everywhere, a massive balcony, high windows and the most brilliant ceiling he'd ever seen. It was covered in nine giant paintings, each framed in ornate gold.

The Banqueting Hall felt grand and old and historical, like something out of a film, not something that actually existed in real life.

'Wow,' both Omari and Edwina exclaimed at the same time as they looked around.

'This used to be part of a bigger palace,' Edwina said. 'But the rest of it got burned down to the ground. This is all that is left. It was used to host masques.'

'What's a masque?' Omari asked.

Edwina sighed and rolled her eyes making Omari regret having asked her.

'A masque is kind of like the plays we put on in drama club, but much fancier. They were often performed in front of kings and queens,' she replied in her know-it-all way.

But this time Omari didn't mind too much. It was actually really cool to hear about the history of this place.

'WRONG!' a voice suddenly bellowed from behind, and they both turned sharply.

Standing by the entrance was

a short man with long curly hair which grew past his shoulders, a very pointed chin and a dark moustache.

Omari suddenly worried that this was some kind of security guard. He thought about the consequences of their break-in and how this guard would probably call the police, who would then call his mum and he'd be locked away in jail in a cell next to Edwina forever. He wasn't sure which part scared him most.

'What?' Edwina said, the quiver in her voice giving away her fear but her arms folded defiantly in front of her, as she regarded the man in front of them.

'I said, you are wrong. Masques are not just little plays. Masques are grand performances. Something you clearly know nothing about,' the man snipped in a snooty voice.

Under different circumstances, Omari might have found anyone dismissing Edwina hilarious and well-deserved, but this man just seemed mean.

Outwardly, Edwina did not seem shaken though.

'I know plenty about grand performances, thank you very much, Mr … who are you, anyway?' Edwina asked.

The man only responded with a creepy smile.

Omari could not wait to leave this place.

He'd proven his point to Edwina now.

'Well, we were just leaving anyway,' Edwina said, as if she could read his mind.

They began walking towards the open wooden doors but then suddenly there was a deep whooshing sound as the doors slammed shut right before them. What followed was the distinct sound of several locks clicking into place.

Omari's heart began to thump rapidly in his chest as Edwina rushed towards the doors and tried to wrench them open with her hands.

But it was no use. They were locked in. They both turned to the man, who was still grinning disturbingly as he stared at them. Omari felt his heart plummet into his stomach.

'W-what is g-going on?' Omari stuttered.

'What is going on is you aren't leaving,' the man said.

'What do you mean?' Edwina asked, her face pinched.

'What I mean is you aren't leaving until you show me what a true masque is. It gets so boring being stuck in here – I wish to be entertained!'

Edwina scoffed, looking at the man in disbelief. Meanwhile, Omari's mind was elsewhere.

'H-how did you l-lock the doors when you

were nowhere near them?' Omari asked, scared to discover the answer.

In response, the man merely let out a low chuckle.

Edwina looked at Omari intently, her eyes motioning to the other side of the room and the doors Omari now saw there.

'You want us to perform for you?' Edwina asked the man.

'For us,' he replied, though, as Omari looked quickly around, there didn't appear to be anyone else in the hall.

Edwina nodded. 'Yes. Well, we'll need to go and prepare,' she said, taking hold of Omari's sleeve. 'We won't be long!'

And then she spun around, pulling Omari with her towards the side of the hall, before switching direction at the last minute and making a beeline for the doors at the other end of the room.

Omari was almost certain they weren't going to make it in time before the strange man somehow locked these doors too, but, to his surprise, when they reached the doors, they swung wide open for them, letting them through.

Relief swelled in his chest as Edwina pulled him towards the nearest staircase.

'Why are we going up? Shouldn't we be going down?' Omari said quietly, as they ran up the steps.

'If you didn't notice, there was no down,' Edwina replied breathlessly as they reached the landing and found another set of doors. 'I'm hoping one of these exits will take us out of here somehow.'

She pushed open the door in front of them, but they quickly realised, to their horror, that they were back in the Banqueting Hall, only this time they were on the balcony peering down at the place they had been stood before.

As they turned to leave, they were met once more with the man, blocking the door, looking at them both with his sinister smile.

'Now, where do you both think you are going?' he asked.

'We told you. We wanted to plan our performance, decide what we're going to do,' Edwina said, but the man held up his hand, stopping her.

'There will be no need for that,' he said, taking a step towards them, forcing them closer to the balcony's edge. 'I will decide what you will perform.'

He stepped forwards once more.

'But to make it a bit more fun, I will tell you a riddle and you must answer that riddle correctly in the form of a masque,' he said.

'A r-riddle?' Omari stuttered.

'Correct,' the man replied.

With their backs now right up against the low

wall of the balcony, and the man getting ever closer, Omari noticed something even stranger about him. The weird shimmering around the outline of his body, like some kind of light was coming ... from within. His smile, while still creepy, now seemed distorted – his mouth a gaping void. Cruel, bulging eyes glared at the pair as he crept slowly closer.

'Here is the riddle,' he said, his voice a whisper but also seeming to pierce right into Omari's skull.

'Begotten of James I, the great King of the North.
Believed he was divine,
to his countrymen he was benign.
Tyrant, traitor and public enemy,
ruinous to his bloodline.
To his subjects, this foolish king lied.
Now show me how he died ...'

There were a few moments of silence before Omari heard a strange sound coming from the hall below, as though a slow wind was pulsing through the building, quietly at first, before getting louder. Whispering, chattering, ghoulish laughter seemed to rise up towards the balcony. A shiver crept up Omari's spine and as he looked at Edwina, he could tell from her expression that she was hearing and feeling the same thing.

'W-what happens if we don't answer your riddle?' she asked.

The Haunted Masque

At once, a flash of anger appeared on the man's face.

'Well, that isn't an option,' he answered harshly. 'You will perform my masque, and you will perform it now,' he said.

'But what—' Edwina began.

'Do NOT dare to question me!' the man roared. 'And do NOT disappoint me!' And then, in one swift movement, he surged towards the pair, hands outstretched, and, though he didn't touch them, they felt a force coming from him which pushed them both over the edge.

It all happened so quickly. One moment they were standing, the next they were falling. Omari could barely hear Edwina's screams over the sound of his own. They were going to die, oh God, they were going to—

Suddenly, the whole world stopped, or rather, their bodies did. But they hadn't hit the ground … in fact they were still somehow suspended in the air. And below them, now filling the Banqueting Hall which had previously been deserted, they saw a mass of people looking up at them. Cruel expressions, hideous smiles, hateful laughter, and, most terrifying of all, the same light Omari had seen in the man was emanating from them all, casting a bright light.

As Omari looked closer, he realised that these weren't like the kinds of people he saw every day on the streets of London at all. They were dressed in old-fashioned clothes and looked almost ... see-through. They seemed to be apparitions, translucent and fluid, as they began to float around the great hall. *Ghosts!* Omari realised with horror.

He opened his mouth, a scream bubbling from deep inside him, but he found he couldn't utter a sound. There was something lodged in his throat, squeezing tight.

He looked down and nearly passed out at the sight.

There appeared to be small pale fingers, reaching right into his mouth. A ghostly hand on the end of them, coming from the man as he hovered next to him. Edwina, likewise, was held up by the man's other hand which had forced its way into her mouth and was lodged around her voice box. Her eyes bulged in terror as her mouth formed a silent scream.

The man drifted towards the ground, dragging Omari and Edwina with him, the crowd below parted and they landed, upright, on the floor of the Banqueting Hall.

As the man (or ghost, as Omari was now certain) finally released them, Omari let out a large gasp as he felt his lungs able to breathe once again.

He looked at Edwina, whose face was red, her eyes brimming with unshed tears.

'Now, to answer your impertinent question, miss,' said the man. 'If you don't answer my riddle, neither of you get to leave. You will stay here forever and perform masques for me and my guests, and entertain us throughout our eternal existence. Do you understand?'

There was an expectant silence, as the ghostly mob leaned in to hear what was being said. Omari and Edwina could only nod in response.

'Good, good, I'm glad we have an understanding.' The man clapped his hands together, and the crowd in front of them cheered and roared in amusement. They were eager to see a masque in this great Banqueting Hall once again. 'You have two minutes to deliberate and then I want to see a grand performance!'

He shooed them away and turned to join his guests.

'That is *not* a person,' Edwina whispered, stating the obvious once they were alone. 'But we seem to have no choice but to obey his orders. I certainly don't want to stay here for a moment longer than necessary – let alone, for all eternity!'

'But we don't know the answer to his riddle,' Omari said, feeling jitters rush through him.

'Yes, we do,' Edwina replied in a whisper. 'Think about it.'

And so he did.

Begotten of James I ... that means James the I's child ... tyrant, traitor and public enemy ... this foolish king lied ...

'The riddle is about Charles I,' he whispered, remembering the tyrannical king they'd learnt about.

'Yes, we just have to perform his beheading, I think,' Edwina said and then turned to the monstrous man. 'We're ready,' she shouted, with more confidence than Omari knew she felt.

'Excellent!' the man replied, before turning to the audience and calling for quiet. Hush descended on the hall.

'You may begin,' the man announced, with a flourish of his hideous hand.

This was the most important performance of their lives, they had to get it right.

As if in her natural element, Edwina assumed the role of the tyrannical king.

She gestured wildly to the ghostly audience, accusing them of all kinds of wrongdoings. Omari pretended to be members of parliament, as she argued. They then performed a scene of a civil war, the same civil war that apparently led to the King's defeat and execution.

The last scene was, of course, the beheading. Edwina got to the ground as Omari swung at her head.

Once they were done, they both stood in front of the man, who watched them both in silence and then began to slowly clap.

The other ghosts joined in, clapping in a way that did not feel like applause, but sounded like the melodic thumping of funeral drums.

When the man ceased his clapping, the others did too, as if led by his silent command.

'Your masque was satisfactory,' he declared. 'You performed my death well.'

'Your death?' Edwina questioned out loud.

The bearded ghost nodded.

'I am the king they called a tyrant; I am the king whose people turned against him.'

This was Charles I! The king who had been beheaded.

'You're King Charles I?' Omari asked in disbelief. His head seemed pretty intact.

The man nodded.

'If we performed well,' Edwina cut in, 'does this mean we can go home?'

'Hmm,' the King pondered, stroking his beard, while the ghostly crowded bustled around him, whispering and chattering in his ear.

'You promised!' Omari urged, terrified by the look of indecision on the King's face.

'It would appear,' the King said finally, 'that you may have performed *too* well. My guests are reluctant to see you go. You see, we get so bored, and we miss the masques of old ...'

And all at once, Omari and Edwina found themselves surrounded by the ghoulish audience who buffeted them around the hall. As the host of eager, yet terrifying, ghosts closed in on all sides, Omari knew that if they didn't make a break for it now, they would be doomed to an eternity trapped within the Banqueting Hall.

He could feel the crowd squeezing him, his breath becoming shallower as ghostly hands grasped and squeezed. He remembered the power of the King's own hands squeezing his throat as they'd floated above the hall.

He felt something gripping his wrist and, as he tried to shake it off, he realised that these fingers were solid, human, flesh and bone.

'Quick,' hissed Edwina, as she dragged him to the floor.

As the ghosts hovered above them, the pair commando-crawled their way beneath. They could hear the wails of despair as the phantoms swarmed above them, searching for their prey.

Eventually, Omari could see the doors ahead of them which, by some miracle of good fortune, were now open wide. He and Edwina jumped to their feet, running the last few metres just as the ghosts spotted them and began to come towards them in a swelling tsunami.

'Shut the doors!' Edwina cried, as they made it through to the corridor outside the hall. And Omari turned, slamming the door in the faces of the crowd.

'If they're truly ghosts, won't they just be able to come through?' he shrieked.

But as they gasped for breath, all was silent. The noise of the King and his phantom guests disappearing behind the thick wood of Banqueting House's doors.

'I don't think they can go beyond the hall,' Edwina said, catching her breath. 'But let's not take that chance – keep running!'

As Edwina and Omari finally emerged from the

Banqueting Hall, Omari turned back once to gaze at the majestic building one last time. It stood, silent as ever, with construction equipment and warning signs, giving no hint of what they'd encountered within. His gaze caught on one of the tall windows on the first floor, where a small ghostly figure with a pointed beard looked down on him and gave a regal wave of his hand.

***

And so, we leave Omari St Vincent as he makes his way home. The boy who never broke any rules but who, on this occasion, told a lie which he would regret for the rest of his life. He never returned to Banqueting House, and, indeed, found an alternative route to the weekly drama group – one which admittedly took him far out of his way but which meant he wouldn't have to walk in the shadows of the ghostly place.

Omari didn't stop acting, though, and went on to become a leading light in the West End, and later Broadway! Audiences and critics alike would comment on how he graced the stage with assurance and confidence. Little did they know that, for Omari, no other performance would be as terrifying as that which he enacted on that strange night many years ago.

And no audience would ever hold the terror for him as the one he faced in the ghostly Banqueting Hall.

HAMPTON COURT PALACE

Children of the Maze

By Sam Sedgman

'Did you hear?' I leaned across the aisle of the coach and tapped Anouk on the shoulder. 'Hampton Court Palace has the oldest hedge maze in the world.'

'Mm,' said Anouk, picking at her nails.

'What's so fun about a stupid maze?' Freddie asked, opening a packet of crisps in the seat beside her.

'Anouk likes solving puzzles,' I said.

'Ugh, no I *don't*,' said Anouk, rolling her eyes and taking a crisp from Freddie. 'Ross, why would you say that?'

I bit my tongue. Anouk had *always* liked puzzles. We'd been friends since she was five. On her ninth birthday, we'd stayed up all night doing a jigsaw of every character from *The Simpsons*. But since Year 9 started, and our school merged with the one across the Westway, it was like she was a different person. All she wanted to do was spend time with Freddie.

'Nerds like puzzles,' said Freddie, chomping a fistful of crisps with an open mouth. 'Are you a *nerd*, Nouk-Nouk?'

'No, obviously.' Anouk smirked as he elbowed her in the ribs, and she pushed her hair behind her ear. I sat back in my seat.

Hampton Court Palace was a sprawling red brick building on the banks of the river. The tops of its crenellated walls looked like teeth biting into the bright blue sky. We filed off the coach on to the gravel path while Mr Lance leaned on his cane and counted us with a stubby finger.

'I want you all on your best behaviour,' Mr Lance said, scowling. 'This is a *royal palace*. I bring the school here every year and you are to represent the Academy in a good light. Cut that *out*, Freddie.'

'I didn't do anything, sir.' Freddie dropped the handful of gravel he'd been about to shove down Pamela Robinson's jumper.

I held up my hand. 'When are we going to see the maze, sir?'

'*Nerd*,' Freddie whispered. Anouk giggled and I

felt my cheeks go hot.

'At the end,' Mr Lance growled. 'Hopefully you'll learn something today. Now get inside, all of you.' He hobbled towards the gate on his cane.

* * *

'Is it true there are ghosts in the palace?' Anouk asked. Our tour guide grinned as we reached the top of a sweeping stone staircase.

'Oh, *dozens*,' she replied. 'In every part of the estate. In this gallery you might even hear the Screaming Queen.'

'Ghosts aren't real,' I muttered.

'Even non-believers report seeing strange apparitions,' the guide said, as she led us down a gallery hung with heavy green fabric. 'Hundreds of years of history happened here. Murders, plotting, intrigue, heartbreak. The desperate yearning for a child to inherit the throne. Ghost scientists say the memories of these strong emotions sink into the stones of the palace – even into the earth itself – and are replayed to us as phantoms and hauntings.'

'Ghost scientists?' I repeated. But the guide had moved on.

'How do you know it's not real?' Anouk said. 'Wouldn't it be cool if it was?' But before I could answer, Freddie had leapt out from behind a curtain, trying to spook me. I darted out of the way and he tumbled forwards against a table, upsetting a precious-looking vase.

'Whoa!' he said, catching it just as Mr Lance stepped into view. 'Watch out, Ross. Don't shove me!'

'Ross!' Mr Lance's eyes bulged. 'What are you doing?'

'I didn't do anything!'

'You're as annoying to teach as your brother was,' Mr Lance snapped, before hobbling away.

I furrowed my eyebrows and watched him go. Anouk stifled a laugh.

'What's so funny?' Freddie asked her.

'He's lost his marbles,' Anouk whispered. 'Ross doesn't even have a brother!'

***

It was late afternoon when we finally reached the maze. Wind rippled through the leaves of the dark, looming hedges.

'Is that it?' Freddie asked, unimpressed.

'Yes, obviously,' said Anouk.

'I thought it'd be ... *greener*.'

'It's the oldest hedge maze in the world,' I said defensively, 'it's over 300 years old.'

'You can tell,' said Freddie. 'Looks like it hasn't

been watered since.'

I could see what Freddie meant. Parts of the maze looked dry. *Thirsty.* Some of the leaves were brown, and branches poked through bald spots in the hedgerow. I felt like an idiot for trying to make Anouk excited by it.

'The aim of the maze is to find the centre,' Mr Lance called out above the chattering class. 'Once you've found your way, return quickly and quietly to the exit. If you get lost, the bus might leave without you.' He chuckled.

'I'm not going to get lost,' Freddie muttered, folding his arms.

'Not if you stick with me,' said Anouk, grinning. 'I know the secret.'

'What secret?' I asked.

'You can solve any maze if you keep your right hand on the right wall and keep following it,' said Anouk. 'It might not be the quickest route, but you'll never go back on yourself and you'll always end up in the centre.'

'I told you she likes puzzles,' I said to Freddie.

'I heard one of the tour guides say it,' Anouk added quickly. 'Come on, let's get this over with.'

The hedgerows reached above our heads, dampening noise from the rest of the garden. It may have been in need of a good water, but it still loomed thick around us. Its edges pushed in tight, and my jumper snagged on a thorny branch. Freddie marched ahead with Anouk, lost among the chatter of our classmates. I unhitched myself and hurried after them, the passage twisting left and right. Gradually the group thinned out as we filtered on to different paths, and the other children became stray voices and glimpses of school ties through gaps in the leaves. I found myself alone.

'You're not keeping your hand on the wall!'

Through the branches I heard Anouk laughing. I turned right, trying to get closer.

'Nah, I'm not going to get lost,' I heard Freddie's confident reply. I saw a flash of movement beyond the hedge and pressed my hand to the prickly branches, following them. 'The middle's, like … that way.'

'Hey, wait up!' I called to them through the hedge.

'Ross?' Anouk turned. 'Is that you?'

'On your left!' I waved but they couldn't see.

'Where are you hiding?' Freddie turned to his right.

'Your *other* left, Freddie!'

Anouk giggled. 'How'd we get split up so fast?'

'It's this way,' I heard a boy call through the hedge. 'You're going to get lost!'

'No, I'm *not*,' Freddie said, angrily. 'Shut up, Ross.'

'I didn't say anything,' I said.

'You'll never find the middle,' I heard a girl say somewhere nearby. 'It's *this* way!'

Footsteps shuffled past behind me. I turned back but there was nobody there.

'Was that you, Anouk?' I asked.

'No,' she replied. I heard her pushing apart the hedge branches with a rustle, hunting for something. 'Who's there?'

There was no answer.

'Stop creeping me out, you two,' said Freddie.

'We're not,' I said.

'You're *creeped out*?' Anouk asked, a smile in her voice.

'No,' Freddie said. 'It's probably just Pamela playing tricks. We're going to beat you, Pam! Come on, Nouk-Nouk.'

I heard their footsteps running away. I suddenly felt very alone.

'Turn back.'

A breeze ruffled the hedge. Through gaps in the branches, I glimpsed a boy in a school blazer walking along the path beside mine.

'Hello?' I pressed my head closer, following him.

'Turn back, Ross,' the boy beyond the hedge said again. 'Before it's too late.'

Something about his voice made my breath catch in my throat. It was familiar.

The boy disappeared down a path I couldn't reach. I turned a corner, hoping it would lead me back to him, and he appeared again beyond the wall of branches.

'Wait!' I called out. 'What do you mean?'

'It's not safe.' I caught the back of his head before he vanished again. He wore our school uniform but I didn't recognise him. He had red hair, like mine.

'You have to go back, Ross. Before you get lost for good.'

The voice came from behind me. I whirled around and stared at the dark hedgerow. Something was bubbling up inside me, and I felt my heart thud in my chest. I stepped closer to the leaves. 'You can't be …' I whispered, reaching out my fingers to part the branches.

'Don't touch the walls!' The force of the boy's words made me pull my hands back like the leaves had burned them. 'That's how it gets you.'

'*What* gets me?' I asked. 'What do you mean? I don't even know you.'

But I did.

Beyond the edge of the path I saw him walk closer to the wall, catching the fraction of a cheek, an ear through gaps in the leaves.

'Yes, you do.'

My mouth quivered. 'Aidan?'

His eyes pierced mine through the gap.

'Hey, little bro.'

I felt the words like a punch. I rocked back against the hedge, before remembering the boy's warning and jumping off it like a bed of knives.

Aidan.

For a moment I remembered running along the beach with him the summer Mum and Dad took us to France, when I'd stayed alone in a bedroom with a bunk bed. But I *hadn't* been alone.

Children of the Maze

'No,' I muttered. 'That's not ... that's not real.' I staggered down the path and turned blindly down forks in the maze. But it *was* real. I could see it. With each turn, a key moved in my mind.

There he was at Christmas, tearing open wrapping paper. When I walked to school with Anouk, he was a few steps behind us with his friends. He was arguing with me in the back of Dad's car. Blowing out the candles on his birthday cake.

Time unzipped. I remembered.

My foot caught under a root sticking out from the path and I tumbled to the ground, scraping my knees through my school trousers. I felt something moving behind the hedgerow.

'You have to go, Ross.' It was Aidan's voice. 'You don't want to be stuck like the rest of us.'

But I couldn't concentrate on anything but him.

'Where did you go?' I asked, trying to catch sight of him.

'I got lost,' my brother replied. He was a shadow moving through the hedge. 'Listen to me. Don't go near the centre. Find the way out and don't look back.'

'I don't understand. What *happened* to you? I'm taking you with me.'

'I can't leave,' Aidan said. 'When you're outside, it'll be like I was never here. Like it was before.' There was a stillness to his voice. 'It's too late for me.

Please, Ross. Don't let it take you, too.'

'*Take* me?'

Wind rustled the hedgerow and my skin prickled. I tried to wrestle my shoe free from the root but it seemed to tighten. I reached down and tugged it free. The hedges around me bristled. I got to my feet, and felt the tendrils of leaves and branches tickling my sides. It was like they were reaching for me.

'Hurry *up*, little bro,' Aidan said. 'It's hungry.'

I took a few steps back the way I had come.

'Anouk,' I said, suddenly. 'I'm not leaving her.'

'There's no time,' Aidan insisted. 'Get out while you can.'

The hedgerows moved as if swayed by the wind. But the air was still.

'OK, I'll leave. But I don't know the way,' I said.

'Turn left,' Aidan said, sounding relieved. I nodded. And turned right.

'Ross!' I heard Aidan's shout lost somewhere behind me as I darted through the thickening hedges, heading deeper into the maze. Anouk was my best friend. I wasn't going to leave her.

The hedges grew higher and thicker as I pushed further along the path. I hit dead ends and doubled back, stumbling over myself and darting through narrow gaps in the walls that seemed to open like mouths. I heard children laughing somewhere beyond the hedges.

'*Come closer!*'
'*Find the middle!*'
'*Play with us!*'

They weren't from my class. I wondered if they were like Aidan; lost in the maze forever. I tried to ignore them, running for Anouk as fast as I could.

I found her in the centre with Freddie. The heart of the maze was a clearing with a tall tree.

I was shocked to see Freddie had started scratching his name into the bark with something sharp. It looked almost like a shard of bone, though I quickly put that thought out of my mind.

'Come on, Freddie,' Anouk was muttering, clutching her arms round her blazer. 'I'm cold.'

'You mean you're *frightened*,' he chortled.

'Did you hear them, too?' I clutched my knees, panting for breath. Anouk jumped, surprised to see me.

'I didn't hear anything.' She looked away.

The wind picked up, rolling like a wave across the hedgerows. It sounded like a breath.

'We need to get out of here,' I said, pulling Anouk away from the wall. 'Now.'

'Why?' Anouk snatched her hand back but noticed the seriousness in my voice.

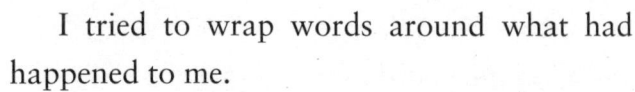

I tried to wrap words around what had happened to me.

'There's something ... here,' I said. 'In the maze. Aidan warned me.'

'Who's Aidan? He sounds like moron,' Freddie scoffed. 'Something here? Like a *monster*? Those voices were just the other kids trying to scare us.'

Anouk was staring at me. 'Aidan?'

I stared back. 'You remember him, too.'

Her jaw clenched, and she turned to Freddie.

'I want to go now,' she said.

'I'm not done.' Freddie was still scratching his name into the tree bark.

'Where did you even get that?' Anouk asked, pointing at the sharp, bone-like object in Freddie's hands. Freddie looked at it, surprised, seeming to consider this himself for the first time.

'Dunno.' He shrugged. 'I found it. Looks a bit gross, actually.'

'Please, Freddie.' I grabbed his arm. 'We have to go.'

A gust of wind howled through the hedgerows, and some branches seemed to dislodge from the side, reaching out like arms.

'So *go*, nerd!' Freddie shouted. 'I said, I'm not done.' He clenched his fist and shoved me away from him. I staggered back, tripping over myself, and fell into the hedge.

Instantly the branches latched on to my shoulders, tightening around me like a seat belt. I tried to move but a root grasped my leg. I tried to cry out but a branch sprouted from the wall and forked around my neck, throttling me.

Anouk screamed as I reached for the bindings, but my arms were useless, fingernails clawing at the thick wood. The branches thickened and tightened around my waist and my neck. I choked, my eyes bulging.

'Ross!' Anouk lunged for me, but tripped over a root that had sprung from the earth and begun wrapping itself round her ankle. Freddie grabbed her out of its way, leaving the white tentacle snatching at air.

'Let's get out of here!' he said.

'But ...' Anouk reached for me, but Freddie grabbed her arm. The branches began heaving me backwards into the hedge.

'It's too late!' Freddie yanked Anouk

towards the path. Leaves slapped over my face, blocking out the light. The last thing I saw was her being dragged down the path, staring at me in horror.

The darkness thickened around me, my throat raw, lungs burning for air. I twitched, barely moving. The vines had sewn together my legs. The earth loosened in a boiling tremor of soil and rock, and the branches sucked me downwards into the churning brown sea.

'Let him go!' It was Aidan's voice. I struggled, unable to draw breath. 'Please!'

But whatever thing Aidan had hoped would respond did nothing. The soil rose around me and my mind began turning to dust.

'Let him make The Bargain!' Aidan shouted.

The branches convulsed at this idea.

'He'll do it,' Aidan insisted. 'He'll be good. I promise. *Better* than Freddie.'

My limbs had grown still.

'Ross, do it,' Aidan pleaded. 'It's the only way. Make The Bargain. Say yes. Say yes.'

The branch around my throat loosened like a belt being unnotched and I heaved in a hoarse, juddering breath.

'*Yes*,' I croaked.

The hedgerow quivered, and the vines spat me

out into the daylight, slackening from my limbs like string. Trembling, I sat up. The hedge that had seized me looked no different than it had before. I was in the centre of the maze but the path out of it had vanished. There was only the tree.

I saw that, alongside Freddie's half-carved name, its bark was carved with dozens of names, many of them faded and healed with time.

'Carve yours,' I heard Aidan say.

I was about to ask how, when I found myself holding what I now knew was an old, sharp piece of bone. My arms burned and I saw my sleeves were in tatters, the skin beneath marked deep with cuts and bruises.

The hedges rustled and seemed to press closer.

'Do it now,' said Aidan. 'Before it changes its mind.'

I staggered to my feet and carved my name into the tree. When I finished the final jagged letter, I felt the hedges soften around me, like a breath being let out. My skin went ice-cold, as if a strong wind were blowing right through me.

I turned and saw the path had reappeared behind me.

'I'm sorry.' Aidan's voice was mournful. 'You should have listened, little bro. Good luck.'

I ran for the path. My trousers were torn, shoes caked in mud, my throat raw. The hedges seemed to sway and bend, the path twisting, the sky teasing me with blue. But then I remembered what Anouk had said. I held out my right hand, holding it just above the pleading leaves. Heart thudding, I squashed every thought in my head except finding the exit, following the imaginary wall like a rope leading me to safety.

I hurried down a long passage, certain it would lead me out until I turned the last corner and saw, like a cruel joke, a dead end. But I wasn't alone there.

'Freddie!' I shouted.

The boy was frantic, tearing at the branches and grunting. He turned round, and the sight of me seemed to scare him more.

'Where's Anouk?'

'You can't fool me,' Freddie said, dried tears on his cheeks. 'It's not real.'

'Where is she?'

'She couldn't keep up.'

'Don't touch the hedge.' I reached for his arm but he pushed me back. 'If you follow the wall with me, we can find our way—'

'That'll take too long!' Freddie yelled. 'I can see the outside. I'm not waiting any longer!'

He tore into the hedge, trying to open its tight knot of wood and climb through to the other side.

The branches rustled and I felt the cold wind pass through me again, like a ghost.

'Don't!' I called out, but it was too late.

The maze reached out for Freddie, thorns biting into his neck. There was a splash of red. A scream. He struggled but the branches gripped his limbs so tight they turned white and purple. With a snap, the wood folded him into the hedge. There was a gargling sound, a blast of hot wind, and nothing left but a spray of dark drops on the ground where seconds ago a boy had stood. The leaves folded shut, wind ruffling them like fur.

I turned away and vomited. Freddie was gone.

I ran. The maze was quiet now. It felt smaller. Only a few moments passed before I emerged into the little lawn in front of the entrance where the rest of my class were sitting on the grass looking bored.

Anouk was on a bench by the flowerbeds, head in her hands, crying.

'There you are,' Mr Lance said, walking briskly towards me. I ignored him, running straight to Anouk. She jumped when I put a hand on her shoulder.

'What happened in there?' Pamela Robinson was sitting beside her, trying to comfort Anouk. 'Ross, your clothes are all ruined. Did you try and climb through a hedge?!'

Something shifted in Anouk's eyes, and a sob fell from her mouth but turned into a laugh.

'Are you—' I started to ask.

'I'm all right,' she interrupted, wiping her eyes. She smiled. 'Just got scared.' She cocked her head. 'Why are you so filthy?'

'Now that you're all back, I think we can go to the bus,' Mr Lance said, clapping his hands together.

'But we're *not* all back,' I protested. 'Freddie's inside, he … the maze, it …'

'Who's Freddie?' asked Anouk.

I stared at her, dumbfounded. I felt dizzy.

'The maze *ate* him,' I said.

Pamela snorted with laughter. 'You're so stupid, Ross. There's no one in our class called Freddie.'

She linked arms with Anouk and led her with the others towards the drive. I couldn't move. I turned back to the maze, whose hedges seemed so much greener than when we'd arrived, lush and thick and swaying proudly in the deep blue afternoon sky.

'It'll be all right, Ross.' Mr Lance stepped over to me with a kindly smile. 'The whole class is here.'

'But Freddie …'

'Shhh.' Mr Lance pressed a finger to his lips. That's when I saw that his cane, the one he always leaned on so heavily, was now only lightly tucked under his arm – almost as if he didn't need it anymore. He noticed my tattered sleeves. 'It's left its mark on you, hasn't it?'

I looked down at my bruised arms, raw and blistered. They pulsed with pain and heat. Mr Lance nodded.

'It's not an easy bargain to keep,' he said. 'But you will, one day. When it calls for you.'

The wind ruffled the hedges again. I shivered. And he led me to the bus with the others.

* * *

But all that was 20 years ago. The bruises never went away, no matter how many doctors Mum and Dad took me to. They itched, and burned, and in the night I thought I heard them whisper. It is worst in summer, when the hedges are dry and hungry.

'Everybody off the bus, single file,' I say, watching my class gather on the gravel. 'I don't want any silly behaviour today.'

A young girl puts up her hand.

'Sir, will we get to go to the maze?'

'At the end,' I tell her, the scars in my arms prickling with excitement. 'You'll all get to go inside.'

The maze is hungry again. And it needs to be fed.

KEW PALACE

A Braid Of Seeds

By Joseph Coelho

Grandad doesn't talk much about the time he worked at Kew Palace. He would always say I wasn't old enough to hear about it, said it was too scary, said 'Leave your grandfather alone' and then, with a laugh, would say his favourite Jamaican saying: 'Duppy know who fi frighten, an' who fi tell good night.' That's basically his way of shutting me up, of telling me to stop bullying him into telling his story.

But this last summer, while we planted seeds in the community garden, something changed. I was telling him about a history project I was doing at school, about a story I wanted to tell, and he started to open up. Slowly at first, a bit like a flower-bud opening in the Sun, he started to reveal more and more of his story.

It's an unbelievable story, but my grandad is a serious man – he don't play, or mess about, or lie. And he definitely wouldn't lie to me, his favourite granddaughter. 'Melody,' he says. 'I'm going to tell you my story. Though it might scare you, it's important that you hear it, and hear it well.' This is his story, and how he told it to me.

***

Kew Palace might close over winter, but the garden within the walled grounds still needs to be tended. The leaf mould and manure from the royal estates spread, earth dug and turned, old foliage burned. The work never stops. When my grandad was still a young man, this walled garden is where he worked – it sits like a royal island within the larger grounds of Kew Gardens. Long before he met my grandma, it was a temporary job before he went off to do a botany degree to write papers like the ones that had inspired his love for plants. The job came with a small flat in the palace basement – it was the 1960s and finding a place to rent was hard, especially as a black man living in London, so this job was a no-brainer. Grandad said, 'Other than your grandmother, the plants in those gardens gave me my greatest joy ... apart from you, of course. Oh, and your mother,' he added, winking.

Then, he told me about the box. He had found it in a far corner of the palace's enclosed garden, behind a stump, all that remained of an ancient yew that had recently died. He'd been digging deep, creating a paving slab box to plant a fig tree. 'You cannot just plant fig trees into the ground, Melody,' he said. 'They grow too big, too wild. They need a living coffin to keep them contained.'

The sound his spade made when hitting the box was so deep and hollow, that at first he thought he *had* hit a coffin. The box was small. A dark, tropical hardwood box, hardly touched by time. The metal lock, however, was a corroded red scab. Without thinking, he took it to his shed and set a hammer and chisel to it. The box was lead-lined and within it were letters and seeds – so many seeds – some that Grandad recognised, some he did not. Definitely millet and sorghum, and a dried twig that might have once been a tuber of some kind.

A Braid Of Seeds

He tried to read the letters but the hand was in that fine looping writing of the olden days and therefore impossible to an untrained eye. Besides, something in him warned against even trying to decipher them. He noted a broken red wax seal and thought that maybe he should have sought help before charging in with a hammer and chisel; this was, after all, royal ground.

Something dark was lying at the bottom of the box. Grandad picked it up carefully. It looked like wool, maybe the soft, silken fibres of a plant. But as he held the thumb length segment in his fingers, he found the texture was familiar. He turned it over and with a shout dropped it back in the box. It was braided, it was hair – very much like his own.

He called the management team for the palace, but it was Friday and no one picked up. He left a message on the answering machine, his voice shaking when describing the find. He didn't know if this was due to him having broken open the box and possibly upsetting an important historical artefact or because the contents unnerved him. Questions ran through his head the rest of the day – who wrote the letters? Why was the box filled with seeds, and why was there a piece of black braided hair within?

And why was it buried? He placed the box under his bed and busied himself with the day's work.

There were several huge pots that needed replanting with new bulbs. Grandad would often layer flowers, creating a pot that would be continuously in bloom once the palace reopened. He felt like he had the world in his pot – from the tulips that originally came from Central Asia, to the daffodil bulbs placed above them that were first grown in North Africa, to the final layer of snowdrops from the Middle East. When he was done, one bulb would bloom and replace another in turn, quietly showcasing all the beauty of the world.

The bulbs took his mind off the December chill and overcast sky that had lain overhead like some terrible weight for too long. He couldn't remember the last time he'd seen blue sky or even sunlight. In the back of his mind, he could feel his attention drawn to the box of seeds and that piece of braided hair beneath his bed. He could feel his mind weaving a narrative together.

The hair was undoubtedly from a black person, but how had it been removed and why? And why was it placed in a box with seeds? The letters were sure to reveal something of the mystery, but he felt a dread lurking there; a knowing that this was some horrible relic from the days of the slave trade.

He had read how the palace's former owner, King George III, had, as a teen, written an essay about how terrible the slave trade was, but that he also spent many years as an adult failing to help the abolitionist cause, believing sugar would be too expensive without slave labour. It was, though, his signature that ultimately gave royal consent to abolition ... eventually. Grandad also knew from his own studies that the king would receive samples from botanists travelling all over the world. Was this box and its contents some sample that needed to be buried? A reminder of a status quo that King George III had let run to seed?

***

That night, Grandad's sleep was troubled. When he did drift off, he heard an echoing *thump, thump, thump*, that had him jolting upright and sweating in the night, throwing off the covers in a daze, only to find the ripping chill of the December air and silence. It was a Friday night, so in his half-sleep, half-waking state he put the noise down to the London traffic, muffled and far off, and eventually he fell back to sleep.

On Saturday morning he was groggy, but still he headed to Mario's, the local cafe where the owner knew him and his order. Grandad could just sit down and his (extra-large) fry-up would magically appear. He'd normally chat with Mario but on this day he remained silent, every sound coming from the rumbling traffic brought to mind the *thump, thump, thumping* that had awoken him the previous night. As a rule, Grandad didn't work on Saturdays, preferring to walk off his breakfast taking in the sights of the larger Kew Gardens and chatting with the gardeners he knew there. But on this day, as he walked, every noise was a reminder of the thumping, every plant brought to mind the seeds in the box and, of course, the length of braided hair.

Saturday night was more restless than the night before. The thumping had awoken him several times and now he swore the sound lingered beyond that period where dreaming and waking knot. But he couldn't be sure it wasn't all in his head and the eerie silence that followed sounded heavy, like it only existed because of those thumps.

Grandad goes quiet before telling me this next bit. 'When trouble catch you, picknie shirt fit you,' he says. Which means that when you're in trouble, anything will do – you'll find comfort wherever you can. He told me that he dreamed of his mother that night, her fingers in his hair, yanking and pulling and braiding. He hated having his hair braided and, even now, though his hair is long, he prefers to keep it in a grey Afro around his head rather than braiding it.

In his dream, his mother's fingers offered some small comfort, but then the pain came. He was crying out, wanting her to stop, just like he did as a child, and he could feel the tightness of his scalp where her fingers worked. He was in front of a mirror and could see his childhood self at about the same age as me, maybe 14 years old, tears running down his face. But behind him was darkness. He could not see his mother, just her hands coming out of the shadows working his hair, too quickly. Were they even her hands? They were big ... too big and calloused and scarred and they yanked and pulled with a strange urgency. The pain was becoming unbearable and a yell tore out of him, waking him out of sleep. His head throbbed. He reached up to touch his scalp – it was tender. It felt wrong. He got up shakily, stumbled to the bathroom, turned on the light. One side of his head had been completely braided by unknown hands.

Grandad spent the morning brushing out his hair, trying to convince himself that he had braided it as he slept. But, of course, that would be impossible. He had never been very good at braiding – I have the proof from the one time he tried to do mine and Mum had to do it all over again.

He even toyed with the idea that his tossing and turning in the night had maybe knotted his hair to resemble a braid, but there's no way that could happen ... but the alternative did not bear thinking about.

'Melody, I don't mind telling you ... I was scared,' he said.

He rang the number of the palace managers again. He knew no one would answer on a Sunday but he was desperate, and ringing made him feel like he was doing something to get the box gone. He moved it from under his bed into one of the many garden sheds; the one furthest from the palace. As he busied himself throughout the day, removing the dry and dead foliage from the last season, his attention kept being snagged by that thumping noise. He could never quite track it to one place – and his scalp remained tender from the braids that had appeared there.

He told me he dreaded the idea of going to bed that night. He worked hard in the daytime in an effort to tire himself out, and it worked – he fell asleep straight away. But the dreams, and the tossing and turning, began almost immediately – dreams of thumps that woke him up every time he drifted off, dreams of fingers curled tight into his hair, dreams of seeds. At around 2 a.m., the tossing and turning and dreams finally got the better of him. The thumping noise was not in his head … it was sounding much clearer than all the other times. It was coming from outside, it was coming from the garden.

He wondered if one of the garden gates had been left open to be played by the wind? He put on a dressing gown and slippers and wearily made his way up from the basement flat.

He didn't like the palace at night, it was too big, too echoey, too full of memory and history. It was here that King George III had suffered his 'madness', it was here that Queen Charlotte had died. When in his flat he could pretend that the space was smaller, pretend that beyond his door was a bustling street or a corridor filled with other front doors leading to other flats filled with families and neighbours, instead of a maze of endless, empty, waiting rooms.

The cold of the garden made him gasp, the thumping had got louder. At the threshold of the garden, on the flowerbeds he knew so well, lay a darkness and a mist making the space unrecognisable. Was the compost in that corner? Were his fruit trees by that wall? He strained his eyes and ears to look and listen, to find the source of the thumping. He dared one foot and then the other from the doorway to the darkness of the path beyond.

As he walked the ground seemed to pitch and wave, causing him to stumble and lurch like going through a haunted house at a funfair. A new sound joined the *thump, thump, thumping* – a sound of groaning and crying on the wind, the sound of voices speaking languages he didn't understand, the sound of waves crashing and snarling.

'I tell you, Melody, I know that trouble nuh set like rain, but this trouble had been goading me for days now so I knew something wasn't right. I knew something was coming.' Grandad goes quiet as he tells me this, tells me of the shock he had that night.

***

He tells me that the mist thickened and soon he wondered if it was the gravel of the garden path he walked on or something else. The sound of waves and crying grew stronger – and behind it all that

thump, thump, thumping. Grandad followed the sound but his legs felt unsteady, his head swayed, and he was falling. The ground that came up to meet him was not path, was not garden, it was wood and ship and slop and wet and mess and dark and he was surrounded by bodies in the bowels of a tossing ship.

African slaves were on their backs and packed tight, chained and manacled, crying and screaming, begging and vomiting. He wanted to help, wanted to free them all, but fear sank into him unlike anything he had ever experienced, a fear that scratched into his bones. He ran from the horror, unable to take in the hellish picture.

There were stairs up ahead and he fled to them, scrambling up on to the deck of a night-knotted ship. And here the thumping was loudest, here it rang through the night … *Thump, thump, thumping.* High up at the back of the ship, two African women were chained by a huge pestle and mortar, their heads matted in shadow, slamming massive wooden pestles into the huge wooden bowl of the mortar whilst another chained slave poured in the rice, removing the husk so that there was food for their torturous journey. As he stared at this scene, the two women stopped what they were doing and looked down towards him with black hollow eyes and silent screaming mouths.

Grandad says he has no memory of how he got back into bed. The dread and fear he felt woke him suddenly the following morning and refused to fade, even with the morning Sun and the ordinariness of wellies, turning the compost heap and pruning the fruit trees. He forced himself to believe he had imagined everything – the thumping, his braided hair, the vision of the ship, all just dreams ... terrible dreams.

* * *

A Miss Wilson, an archaeologist, arrived around midday on Monday. She was a short woman who laughed at the end of every sentence, whether what she said was funny or not. She wore her hair in a short Afro, tied with a bright silk.

'We just got your message, ha-ha. About finding something in the garden, hee-hee. Let's see what we've got shall we? Ha-ha.'

Grandad collected the box and laid it carefully on the desk, telling her nothing of the contents. It felt heavier than before, much heavier.

'Let's take a looky-loo, shall we?' said Miss Wilson, removing a pair of white gloves from an overly stuffed bumbag. She gave Grandad an accusing look on seeing the busted lock – sighing loudly before lifting the lid and removing the documents.

'Is everything here? Hee-hee,' she asked, not making eye contact though the accusation was clear. Grandad nodded and peered over her shoulder into the box where the length of braided hair lay.

'This is fascinating. Ha-ha. Incredible,' she said, removing a magnifying glass from her pocket and squinting at the letter through it. 'This is a correspondence sent from a botanist to the royal household of the time – so to King George III, ha-ha. We know that King George III regularly received specimens from botanists, he had such an interest in flora ... Ha. This botanist was ... erm ... visiting slave plantations and investigating the flora there. It's a ... a ... an inventory of seeds from his findings ... and, oh dear. Ha.'

She went silent for an uncomfortably long period of time, reading and re-reading the documents and finally, gingerly fingering the contents – the seeds, the gnarled root, the braided hair. Grandad wanted to warn her about the hair but it was too late. One end of the braid had become loose, and grains of rice fell from it, tinkling into the lead lining of the wooden box, and Miss Wilson gasped. Grandad sat her on a chair when she appeared unsteady on her feet, he left to get her a glass of water and on his return, he found her crying.

'They took the seeds to grow and braided them into their hair,' she said. 'They had no idea where they were going, or when they would get there, so they took any seeds they could from the food they were fed onboard the ships. The unmilled rice, any small uncooked tubers, millet seeds, sorghum – whatever they could get – and hid them; braided them into their hair for safekeeping, so they could build a life beyond enslavement.'

She started to read from one of the letters from the botanist, dated 17 March 1790 – it was a diary extract. *'We have been at sea for 34 days. The inhumanity and brutality on-board is unlike anything I have ever witnessed. There was a revolt three nights ago, the second of our journey so far. Two African women died as a result, and one member of the crew jumped overboard and drowned. The revolt was in response to crew discovering that one of the slave women, employed in preparing the rice on-board in the pestle and mortar, had taken a handful of seed and braided it into a fellow slave's hair, presumably for hoarding. She was whipped, and her braid cruelly removed. The slaves very nearly took control of the ship.'*

Miss Wilson wiped her eyes and stared at Grandad. 'We have always known about the risks women took to hide seeds, but never found a record of such a brave act. The transatlantic slave trade that brought millions of pounds into Britain by royal charter, all the while the enslaved gave their lives. These women took incredible risks to have hope, to ensure they had seeds to survive escape – we still see the results of their efforts to this day. In Suriname, in South America, there are communities descended from escaped slaves, communities made possible because of seeds. Communities that grow crops that originate from Africa – yam, sorghum, pigeon peas. These brave enslaved women created a food system that still survives today – a system that avoids disease and pests, a system that will likely have to replace the way we farm today, a system that may save us all.'

She began crying again, all joy had been drained from her. 'This is an incredibly important find,' she said. 'This is a story that must be shared.'

In the weeks that followed, Grandad found himself pondering the lead lined box found in Kew Palace gardens. He wanted to do something, to somehow honour those that had lost their lives. He contacted Miss Wilson and secured a few of the seeds from the find that had since been catalogued and labelled. He didn't expect them to grow – Miss Wilson had said they were likely to be unviable – but he didn't care, he had to try. He chose a large flowerbed in the centre of the garden at Kew Palace, turned the soil with a hand rake, adding compost, and finally watered it. The seeds grew. The bed became a living monument to the slaves that had risked everything, that had had everything taken from them. In that bed, he grew their seeds and ensured for years after that visitors to the palace knew their story.

Grandad gave up the living quarters in the palace – he loved working there, loved the gardens, but was now hungry to connect with others. He found an apartment in North London, with neighbours and overheard laughter and arguments and music. The community garden there was a surprise, somewhere he could take his experiences and make them mean something, do something that went beyond him, that took his life beyond the palace and its memories. It was nestled at the edge of an estate in his new neighbourhood, built on a piece of disused land, its small, ramshackle fences seemed more for design than security.

Before he knew it, he was not only reworking the large beds of the site but also organising seed swaps and giving talks to visiting school groups. He grew that garden into something incredible, increasing its size when a plot of land became available and, over the years, turning it into something magical. When I came along, he got me to help out, too. He says his gardening passion found a new depth after that experience; an unshakeable pride in the knowledge of what our ancestors have overcome, of the length and risks those enslaved took to survive.

'Melody,' he said. 'I see my love for gardening in a whole new light – something that connects me to them, something I want to share beyond myself ... with you, with everyone. And when the thumping sounds again at night, and sometimes it does, it does not scare me anymore because now I hear more sounds within it. I hear louder and louder the singing and uproar and rage of the enslaved upon those ships. I feel I understand the voices of the many languages being spoken to me of Mandinka, Mende and Gola, of Igbo and Yoruba. And I feel more than anything the desire to tell their story.'

BANQUETING HOUSE

THE SUNDIAL

By Alexia Casale

London, 1622

John Webb, being almost 12 years of age and having yet to make his mark on the world, was having a normal (boring) morning when Destiny called his name. With the rest of the household stricken by loose bowels, there was no one else to deliver a letter from his father to the Surveyor of the King's Works. Despite the inauspicious reason for John's task, nothing could deny the glory of his destination – Whitehall Palace.

The Sun blazed as John set out in his best doublet and breeches. Soon, he would tread the same ground as kings and queens, adventurers like Sir Walter Raleigh, and spymasters like Sir Francis Walsingham.

Surely, he would return forever changed. The streets were thronged with people. John picked his steps carefully, so he was nearly there before he took in the palace.

It was surprisingly low: a sprawl of large houses and stables on either side of a busy street. Two grand gatehouses marked the north end, with King James's magnificent new Banqueting House rising above it all, the three different types of stone glowing pinkish, honey-gold and grey-white.

A girl about John's age was struggling with a huge leather portfolio. A page broke free and John darted after it. With a lunge, he caught the page just above the surface of a muddy puddle.

'A gallant rescue indeed.'

The man standing before him had a long face, moustache and pointed beard, making it seem longer still. His clothing was plain in design, but the sumptuous fabric caught the light in fawn and gold. His keen eyes were full of cleverness.

John proffered the rescued page only to pause as he took in the astonishing tracery of delicate lines. Here, in his hands, was the majestic Banqueting House in every detail.

'Are you going to give Inigo's plan back?'

The girl was glaring at him, hands on hips, though the man – this had to be Inigo Jones,

Surveyor of the King's Works – was smiling.

'What Anne means is "Thank you",' Inigo said ruefully.

John held out the page with a bow. 'It's a work of art. To draw this and so create that …' John gestured at Banqueting House. 'My father said you studied the ancient buildings of Italy. Centuries hence, men will surely study yours in turn.'

Inigo's eyes crinkled. 'A man may dream. At least my Banqueting House, being stone instead of wood, should last longer than its predecessors.'

John held out his letter. 'From my father, seeking to supply your next royal commission.'

Inigo took the sealed fold of paper. 'I wonder if you would await my reply. I have business for an hour, but surely you'd enjoy a tour with Anne?' When John nodded, he marched away.

'When Inigo says an hour, he means three.' Anne grinned. 'Still, it'll give me time to show you around, then we can look at Inigo's costume designs for the masque ball King James has ordered to celebrate the completion of Banqueting House.'

Grabbing John's wrist, she set off towards Court Gate, then dragged him across a great courtyard and through a passageway. She turned just before a long gallery, towing him into—

'The Privy Garden? We can't play in the King and Queen's private garden!'

Anne laughed, skipping over to a huge stone sundial. 'I can't believe they're replacing this. It'll be gone later today so they can assemble the new one in its place.' She traced a hand across the stone. 'The inscription is by William Fowler, a famous *makar* – that's Scottish for poet. The new one's designed by a mathematician. It's meant to be very clever about the stars and things, but it looks ridiculous – all these bits sticking out.' She made a face.

John bent closer to the inscription. 'Is it English?'

'I think it's Latin, but the letters are so fancy I can't make out all the words.' She pointed at a curling shape. 'Is that an S or a F?'

John tipped his head. 'Would your father know?'

'You mean Inigo? He's my uncle. Though sometimes people assume otherwise.' She wrinkled her nose. 'He would know, but I can work out most of it.' She circled the sundial, fingers running around the edge as she chanted.

'*Vera monstro, micante radio, sero memores, tempore curae, auspice plebo, velut desolat hora gradu, tempus enpetur.*'

John followed, echoing her. They were laughing as they circled a third time, just as the bells began to ring the hour.

Chime. Chime. Chime.

But the third chime was sharp and discordant. The notes rippled through the air with the force of a buffeting wind. Anne tumbled to the ground, while John braced himself against the plinth, rubbing his forehead. The world seemed to whirl around them.

'How many times did we go round?' Anne moaned as she pulled herself up. 'My head's spinning.'

John reached out to help, then froze.

'What's wrong?' Anne asked, seeing his expression. Then she realised what John was staring at.

Banqueting House had vanished.

Anne whipped around. The great gatehouses behind the garden wall were still there, the latticework windows in the octagonal turrets of Holbein Gate reflecting the sky. But the design of the garden had changed. The surrounding buildings around the great stone gallery were different, too: lower with smaller windows, the glass thick and murky rather than clear and fine.

'Can you see this, too?' whispered Anne.

'What happened?' John swallowed. 'Are you a witch?'

Anne glared. 'It wasn't me! I've done the chant before and nothing happened. If anyone's a witch, it's you!'

'I'm not! I just echoed you.'

Voices sounded nearby. Anne dragged John into a doorway.

'I thought you said we wouldn't get in trouble coming here!' John hissed.

'That was before the whole world went … wrong,' she hissed back.

They pressed close to the brickwork, peering out.

A sharp-faced man with a jutting beard and moustache came marching briskly down the stone gallery. He was clothed in black velvet, a round lace ruff wrapping his throat and wrists.

Anne and John gaped at his funny, old-fashioned clothing. A tight black cap cupped the back of his head.

'It's like he's from my grandfather's time,' John said wonderingly.

Anne scowled at him. 'Of course he is! How else would the buildings be so different? We're in the old Palace – we've gone back in time.'

'But that's not …' John trailed off. It clearly was possible. 'What year do you think it is?'

Anne surveyed the buildings around them, pointing at the furthest gatehouse visible behind the garden wall. 'Inigo says the King's Street Gate was built about 70 years ago, so it can't be longer ago than that. I don't think that man's clothing was that old.' She shook her head. 'It doesn't matter. The important thing is finding our way back to our own time.'

With the man out of sight, she hurried back to the sundial. Reaching out a trembling hand, she laid it on the stone.

'The inscription's gone!'

John rushed over. The stone was unmarked. 'We must have gone back to before they put the words on. What if it doesn't work without them? I don't remember—'

'I do! We didn't say the whole inscription anyway. So long as we chant the same words …'

She began circling the sundial, speaking loud and clear so John could echo her as he followed.

'*Vera monstro, micante radio, sero memores …*'

When they'd gone round three times, they turned to where Banqueting House should have been glowing against the sky. There was nothing but ribbons of cloud.

John's shoulders slumped. 'Maybe we have to go in the opposite direction?' he suggested.

Off they went again, but it was no use.

Anne growled, hands curling into fists. 'Something must have been different the first time. It's not the words or the direction so …'

John's eyes widened. 'The bells were ringing before. What if that's part of the spell? If we wait—'

'We can't wait here. If someone from this time sees us lurking, they'll think we're spies and throw us in the Tower with the other traitors! They might chop off our heads!'

Suddenly, they heard the sound of approaching footsteps. They hurried back to the doorway, just as two figures came into view.

A richly dressed lady stepped into the gallery at the head of the garden. Her red hair was sculpted into an ornate halo, studded with pearls and gems. At her side stalked the sharp-faced man in black.

Anne and John stared at each other.

'Queen Elizabeth!' mouthed Anne.

'What news from your spy in the court of my would-be heir?' Queen Elizabeth asked as she sailed into the garden.

'The man must be Spymaster Walsingham!' John mouthed back.

'Fowler enjoys good favour as both secretary to his patron's wife and court poet,' replied Walsingham.

Alexia Casale

'Fowler? The one who wrote the verse on the sundial?' John whispered.

'His patron shares Fowler's passion for poems with hidden anagrams,' said Walsingham dourly. 'Given James's obsession with witches, it's a wonder he doesn't believe Fowler to be hiding spells in his little poem puzzles.'

Anne leant forwards to catch his words only to squeak as she stumbled.

'Who goes there?' Walsingham called sharply.

'We can't run – we have to stay near the sundial,' John whispered urgently. 'I'll go out and—'

'No.' Anne glared him. 'We're in this together.' She raised her chin defiantly and stepped out on to the path, John at her heels.

John scraped a deep bow, while Anne curtsied.

'We didn't mean to disturb you, Your Majesty. We were just playing.' Anne did her best to look innocent, but she might as well have shouted, *We're up to no good!*

'Come here!' the Queen commanded.

Anne and John crept forwards, stopping by the sundial.

Queen Elizabeth frowned as she surveyed them. 'You look like foreigners and yet you speak a fair English tongue. How do you come to be lurking in my garden – and who do you plan to tell about what you have heard here?' Her voice was mild, but her eyes were cold.

'Not a soul,' breathed John.

Anne nodded. 'We'd be in trouble.'

'Indeed, since the penalty for treachery is execution,' hissed Walsingham.

'But loyal friends need have no fear.' Queen Elizabeth gifted them a beneficent smile. 'You may have listened to my conversation with Walsingham, but since we are friends now, it can be our secret.' She winked. 'So, tell me your names, little friends, then we shall sit and get to know each other while Walsingham,' she flicked the spymaster a glance, 'sends for … sweetmeats. We speak of great matters and that requires sustenance!'

Although the Queen's tone was warm, the pause before the offer of sweets saw John and Anne take a fearful step back.

Then, without warning, the world trembled. The buildings twisted and blurred. Anne stumbled into John, sending him staggering sideways towards the sundial. His hand went straight through the stone. He snatched his fingers back.

'Witchcraft!' Walsingham gasped.

Before their eyes, the sundial blurred into two. One solid and plain, the other translucent with gilded words carved into the stone.

Anne reached out to the plain stone sundial. It was real and solid, but the other one wavered, blurring sideways as if it were moving.

The sky above the garden wall flickered and, suddenly, Inigo Jones's grand masterpiece glowed in the sunshine once more – a glimpse of their own time. Anne and John felt hope flood through them.

Then Banqueting House swayed, distorted and vanished again. A moment later, it was back as a mere outline. A drift of cloud sailed through it.

'What devilry do these witches bring upon us?' the Queen whispered, raising her hands as if warding away an attack. 'Guards!' she croaked. Then, 'GUARDS!'

Anne bolted. John pelted after her.

'The bells didn't ring so how did that happen?' John shouted as they ran.

'They must be moving the sundial in our time!' Anne shouted back. 'If it's the anchor for the spell, now it's no longer in the same place in both times—'

'Time's coming unstuck,' John finished.

They made for a doorway but it vanished, to be replaced by a wooden wall. Anne and John skidded to a stop. A moment later, the doorway was back.

'What if it changes back to wood as we go through?' John asked, voice wavering.

Anne glanced back. Walsingham was mere yards away.

She grabbed John's hand and dragged him through the doorway. Their feet struck flagstones.

They were in a cool, brick-walled room. But then the ground lurched beneath them again and the flagstones were replaced by beaten earth and reeds, the brick walls by wood and whitewashed plaster.

Something melted through the wall – Walsingham's face, and a hand reaching for them.

With screams they fled, Anne leading the way as best she could through the changing network of buildings.

'Our sundial is the one with Fowler's inscription, but how do we find it before the bells chime when there are guards everywhere?' John panted.

'They're replacing it,' Anne gasped back, 'so they'll take it out on the street. We just have to stay ahead of the guards as we make our way out of the palace.'

'What happens if they take the sundial away before the bells ring?'

Eyes widening, they ran even faster.

Hurtling through a door, they found themselves back in the great courtyard. To their left stood Inigo's glorious Banqueting House. Then it crumpled into a low, flimsy structure of wood and canvas painted to look like stone. A moment later, it was a wooden barn. The sudden, jolting changes were making John's head whirl.

'Death to the witches!' someone shouted behind them.

Looking back, they saw Walsingham pointing across the courtyard at them, flanked by men at arms.

Anne and John darted for Banqueting House. When they glanced back, there was no one behind them except a servant in strange attire, staring at them as if they'd popped out of thin air.

Then suddenly he was gone and there was Walsingham – gaining on them fast.

Panicked, they sped up as much as their aching legs and lungs would allow.

John felt a shout of fear leave him as they charged for the doorway into Banqueting House. He squeezed his eyes shut …

They burst into the echoing chamber. Two lines of columns towered up on either side, bearing a ceiling lofty as a cathedral.

This was the Banqueting House of their own time.

Suddenly, it shrank down into a structure of wood and canvas, and they were lost in the past once more. Anne shrieked as her foot sent a bottle clattering away across the floor. The space was filled with the debris of a party.

Then time warped again and they were in the wooden barn. A torch guttered at the far end where a group of men were gathering up dirty reeds from the floor.

A moment later, they found themselves in the wood and canvas structure once more. They slumped against a wooden column.

'This must be the hall from Elizabeth's reign,' Anne whispered. She raised a shaking arm to point at the far end. 'There's a … door there … in our time—'

She screamed as a bony hand shot straight through the column behind them. Gnarled fingers clamped down on John's shoulder.

There stood Walsingham, dark eyes cavernous and glittering. In his free hand, he held a dagger.

Scrambling among the rubbish at her feet, Anne grabbed a platter, slamming the edge into Walsingham's shin. With a howl, he staggered back just as the hall twisted into Banqueting House again.

Anne and John gaped in frozen horror as a stone

column swallowed him, then dashed away before time could distort once more and bring Walsingham back to chase them all over again.

A massive figure reared up in their path. A grotesque boar's head mask covered its face.

They swerved, then stumbled back from a harlequin with a huge headpiece, dangling bells. They clung to each other as towering, cloaked figures circled them.

John flung himself down on all fours and scuttled under the hem of the boar's cloak, escaping out the other side, Anne following as the figures cried out in glee and turned in pursuit, shrieking with drunken laughter.

'It's a masque ball,' Anne gasped as they scrambled away.

'This is Banqueting House, but it's not quite complete in our time. Is this the future?'

'Inigo designed that costume!' Anne panted, pointing into the swirling crowd at a tall man in an even taller crown of blue feathers, bearing a stick with red and orange streamers bursting from it like flames. 'It must be only a month or so after our time!'

Before she could look for more clues, the cloaked dancers disappeared.

Someone cried out.

They whirled to find themselves in the near-empty barn. The servants who'd been clearing the reeds were staring in horror at their sudden appearance. One tumbled backwards, his flailing hand catching the torch and sending it toppling from its bracket. The other men rushed to stamp out the embers, but the pile of reeds was already alight.

'This must be the hall that burned down three years ago. The one Inigo was commissioned to replace!' Anne whispered as they stared in fascinated horror at the fire.

Suddenly the servants were gone and the masque swallowed them once more, cloaks swirling as the crowd bellowed and screeched. Banqueting House reared around them.

'Capture the witch children!' the harlequin roared.

A bear rushed them from the left, while the huge beak of a Venetian plague-doctor mask loomed from the right, red-gloved hands reaching.

Then they were gone and there was Walsingham. Yet, when Anne and John turned to run, the hall ahead was still ablaze.

'Time's running together,' John whispered desperately. 'It's all happening at once …'

Walsingham stalked forwards but now he was aging before their eyes, skin turning grey, the lines on his face deepening, the flesh sagging from his bones until it frayed away in age-blackened scraps. His dark eyes glinted in the bony sockets and his shadow loomed ever taller.

The children backed towards the fire, the heat stinging their cheeks.

'Didn't the old Banqueting Hall burn to the ground?' John croaked. 'We can't go that way!'

'But Walsingham will have us executed as witches! And it's the only way to get to the sundial before the bells ring. Do you want to be stuck in the past? Maybe that', she pointed at Walsingham, 'will happen to us, too!'

Shrieking rang through the hall as the masked revellers surged towards them once more, the boar galloping on all fours, the plague-doctor almost gliding. But Walsingham didn't vanish. Instead, he flowed forwards, dagger in one hand, the other clenched into a claw of bare, blackened bones.

Anne looked at John. He nodded. Together, they ran towards the fire.

The walls crackled with flames. Sparks and ash rained down from the roof while smoke billowed up all around. They leaped over benches, dodging toppled chairs, swerving as columns appeared from nowhere and the Banqueting House of their own time towered over them once more.

Despite the shift to their own time, the smoke was as thick as ever, the fire just as hot against their backs as if all the different versions of the hall throughout time were merging into one.

As they glanced back, they saw Walsingham and the masked revellers burst through the writhing smoke, dozens of hands reaching to grasp them.

Ahead, a blank wooden wall suddenly blocked their way. Then it was replaced by the stonework of Banqueting House. And there, finally, in the left-hand corner, was a door.

Legs and lungs burning, they plunged from thick smoke and searing flames out into sunlight. Clouds boiled in the sky as if time was galloping out of control.

'Which way?' gasped John.

Anne staggered past Banqueting House towards the arch of Holbein Gate. Beyond, in the street, a group of men were lifting the sundial on to a cart.

With a groan, John forced himself into a trot, Anne stumbling beside him.

Chime.

Their eyes met in terror. If they didn't reach the sundial before the bells finished ringing, there would be no escape from their pursuers into their own time. Surely only death awaited if they were captured in the past.

A roar of rage echoed down Whitehall. The black figure of Walsingham streamed towards them, masked revellers swarming beside him, their black and crimson cloaks flying like the wings of demons escaped from hell.

Chime.

John and Anne hurtled towards the gate. As they staggered out the other side, the clouds broke open on a brilliant sunset, painting Whitehall and Banqueting House in crimson.

Chime.

The world twisted as if London were melting and suddenly they were running down a strange black road, painted with odd white and yellow markings. Towering glass buildings reached into the sky, ten times higher than even the great St Paul's Cathedral. Surely such things existed nowhere on earth – at least not yet.

This had to be some future London glimpsed as time unravelled, as the sundial in the past and the sundial in their own time grew even further apart.

In future London, the gatehouses were gone, along with all the rest of the Palace – except for one solitary building. As they glanced back, Banqueting House glowed against the scarlet sky, untouched by time.

Chime.

The clouds closed in and future London vanished, replaced by the London of their own time. The Palace was back, with the King's Street Gate dead ahead. And in front of it, the cart and sundial.

They threw themselves forwards, scrambling into the cart and slapping their hands on to the sundial. Their breath coming in ragged gasps, they squeezed their way around it, chanting desperately.

'*Vera monstro, micante radio ...*'

Chime.

Suddenly everything stilled. The world grew solid beneath their feet. Banqueting House glowed against the sky. Nothing flickered. Walsingham and the masked revellers were gone.

They were home.

'Oi! Where d'you two come from?' cried the nearest worker, staring in confusion.

They scrambled down from the cart as the man started securing the sundial in place. Collapsing on to a crate, they burst into breathless laughter, limp with relief.

'You look as if you've had quite the time together.' Inigo smiled down at them. 'What have you been up to that you've covered your clothes in ash?'

Sitting beside Anne, he sighed as he stared at the sunset above Banqueting House. 'My work pales in comparison to such natural wonder. I hope this crimson light isn't a portend that fire will consume this hall, too.'

John and Anne exchanged a solemn look, remembering their glimpse of future London, with Banqueting House safe amongst the towering glass buildings.

'There may be other fires, but Banqueting House won't be destroyed,' John told Inigo. 'It will last for centuries.'

Inigo laughed. 'From your lips to God's ears.

Now, time for home, though I wager this won't be the last we see of each other.'

'Of course not!' said Anne. 'We're friends now.' She winked.

John winked back. 'We even have a secret.'

Hillsborough Castle and Gardens

IN THIS STILL PLACE

By Sophie Kirtley

1st February 1839
At Sea

Dearest Diary,

Ireland will be my home while Mama and Papa are away and, as I write, the ship is finally approaching shore. Through the fog I can just see Belfast Docks, prickled with red lantern lights – like hundreds of sharp little eyes. I have read that there are more spirits here in Ireland than in any other country in the world – banshees, faery folk, goblins, ghosts …

I see the silhouette of a crane and winches, towering like a hangman's gibbet, all steam and smoke and swaying ropes. They say this is a friendly place, but I feel an edge of threat in the air, like something is awry.

With a jolt and a shudder and the shouting of men, we dock. We have arrived.

1st February 1839, Evening
Hillsborough Castle

Dearest Diary,

The final stage of my long journey has been somewhat eventful.

Cousin Caroline wasn't able to collect me in person from the port, as I had hoped. Instead, she had sent a carriage to bring me to her home at Hillsborough Castle. The way was rough, and the driver in a dreadful hurry. When I asked him if we might pause a while for me to refresh myself, he grew pale and said sharply that 'at all costs' we needed to reach Hillsborough Castle before nightfall.

The winter sky was near dark already, and as the bare-branched trees flailed in the biting wind I tightened my shawl around me and shivered, struck by the hopeless, barren spirit of this land I must soon learn to call 'home'. I remarked at the beauty of the rising moon to the driver. He hurried the poor mare onward at a frenzied pace, his hands so tight upon the reins that his knuckles gleamed white as bone.

As we thundered towards Hillsborough, a freezing fog descended. I could see castle towers silhouetted on a hill, yet to my surprise the driver turned towards a different place. 'But surely that is the castle?' I asked him, pointing yonder.

'No, Miss Nora. That's the fort. This here is the castle.' He pointed to a large house on the village square and we pushed on towards it.

I swallowed my disappointment. Hillsborough Castle was not how I had imagined – it was grand, yes, but I had been hoping that my new home would be a dreamlike fortress with cobwebbed dungeons and towering turrets – a castle quite ripe for adventure. This was not that place, and I sensed already an air of sorrow about it.

The carriage skidded to a halt and I gazed around the foggy courtyard. I saw a movement in the shadows and peered closer.

A boy of around my own age was there, his hair and clothes wet through. He was bent double, head in his hands, and sobbing his poor heart out. All bedraggled and alone.

The driver flung open the carriage door. 'We must help that poor bo—' I began. But the man was in such a rush, he didn't seem to hear me. Or, perhaps, he chose not to.

'Hurry along now, Miss Nora,' he said, his face pale as moon. 'Mustn't be out after dark!'

'But why?' I asked, trotting after him. The man gave no reply.

I looked back through the fog and the boy was gone. Yet for a moment I thought I could still hear his sobs, so faintly … then … nothing … simply the wind …

A pale young maidservant beckoned me from the threshold. 'Come in quick now, miss,' she said as she banged the door shut and drew the bolt across. 'You're not to go out, nor even look out, after dark,' she said, rather impertinently I considered.

'Where is Lady Caroline?' I enquired. Although she is my cousin, we have never actually met. But as she is not many years my senior, I had hoped that a friendship would spark between us at first sight.

To my surprise, I was told that Cousin Caroline was already sleeping, despite the early hour. With the Earl and his parents away on business, I was shown to my chamber where I have since dined alone.

And here I sit, writing, and pondering this most strange and unwelcoming of welcomes. Outside the wild winds howl, but inside the house is so silent and still. Almost as if it is holding its breath, waiting ...

2nd February 1839
The Library, Hillsborough Castle

Dearest Diary,

I am beginning to fear that something is terribly wrong here at Hillsborough Castle.

I still have yet to meet Cousin Caroline; she didn't come to breakfast, nor luncheon and now the day is nearly done. When I asked the young maidservant, Millie, her explanation was: 'Her nerves are bad today, miss.'

So I have spent the day alone in the library, my only company being the old Wolfhound, Sancho, who snoozes by the fire. I did try to read but when I picked up a newspaper that lay upon the side table, I saw its date was October 1837 — more than one year ago!

I gazed out into the gardens; a thorn of loneliness pressed in upon my chest, but I tried not to feel its sharpness. A thin fog had gathered on the lawn and darkness was approaching. I watched a scattering of crows settle on a knotted treetop and suddenly the strangest feeling came over me. An icy, shivering feeling, and a sense of someone watching me.

My heartbeat quickened. I glanced behind me to see if perhaps my cousin had entered the library, but no – only Sancho who slumbered still. I turned back to the gardens, my eyes darting from shadow to shadow.

Was somebody out there? In this still place …

Suddenly, the library door opened and my heart flipped.

'Sorry, Miss Nora.' It was Mrs Bell, the housekeeper. 'We would've knocked if we'd known you were in here …' She and Millie went about their business, lighting the lamps in silence. Then, as Millie drew the heavy curtains closed, I noticed she had turned her head from the window and squeezed her eyes tight shut.

She caught me staring and, blushing, she murmured, 'Best not to look …'. I wasn't able to quiz her further as I saw Mrs Bell deliver a sharp look in Millie's direction, and then the pair were gone.

Alone once more, the old dog stares at me with his amber eyes.

'What is going on, Sancho?' I whisper, stroking his rough grey fur. 'Why is everyone in Hillsborough so nervous and strange?' The coals shift in the fire sending up a devilish hiss of sparks. The fearfulness here is spreading it seems, for my heart feels an icy chill. Yet I know not what it is that I fear …

3rd February 1839
Hillsborough Castle

Dearest Diary,

It is nearing midnight. I write by candlelight while all others sleep. I myself am sleepless – for reasons which shall soon become clear. Let me explain …

This evening at bedtime I was in my chamber, just about to write of my silent, lonesome day, when I realised that I had foolishly left my diary in the library. I crept swiftly through the slumbering Castle to retrieve it and had just snatched it up when I heard footsteps approaching in the corridor. A wave of panic hit me as I realised my own impertinence – I had no permission to be roaming the rooms by night, I was a guest here. Not knowing what else to do, I slid behind the thick velvet curtains and tried to still the noise of my thumping heart.

Presently I heard the door open and, peeking

between the curtains, I saw a woman whom I recognised as Cousin Caroline. She was dressed in night clothes, her hair loose and unkempt, a troubled look in her eye. By her side padded Sancho, his eyes aglow in the fading firelight.

'Oh, Sancho!' sighed Cousin Caroline. The dog gave a gruff bark in response. 'What will become of us? Whatever are we to do?'

My curiosity was piqued – perhaps my cousin would reveal the Castle's fearful secret …

Sancho, however, had picked up my scent. My heart tightened as his claws click-clacked closer. His grey muzzle appeared, snuffling beneath the curtain, and I drew back my feet. Then, to my surprise, the friendly dog began to growl.

'What is it, boy?' Cousin Caroline's voice was strained. I winced, eyes closed, waiting for her hand to whip back the curtain and find me here. But instead, I heard a soft cry and fleeing footsteps. Cousin Caroline was gone.

I felt my heart melt with relief. Sancho was now behind

the curtain too, and he had started to whimper.

'Don't worry, Sancho,' I said gently, extending my hand. 'It's only me – Nora! We're friends, remember?'

But Sancho's eyes were fixed on the window behind me.

I turned to the glass and drew back with a cry.

A shadowy figure stood outside on the moonlit lawn, peering in.

Pale skin. Dark eyes. Wet hair.

It was the boy I had seen in the courtyard. I gasped in surprise. His eyes bored into mine, but this time he wasn't crying … his stare was full of fury.

'W-what is it? W-what is wrong?' I stammered, clouding steam upon the glass.

The boy stepped closer, narrowing his eyes. Sancho's growl deepened. I began to back away from the window but the boy held me in his glare and pointed a long pale finger straight at me … like an accusation …

Sancho barked then, rearing on to his hind legs, clawing at the glass. From nowhere, a wild wind gusted and the windows rattled. Heart pounding, I staggered back and my skirts must have become entangled in the curtains, for I tumbled with a clattering din.

I looked up, dazed, as the library door was flung open. There stood Millie. 'Are you all right, Miss Nora?' she asked kindly.

In This Still Place

'Quite all right,' I replied, aware of my own flailing ridiculousness as I tried to get back to my feet.

'Let me give you a wee hand there, miss,' said Millie, biting back a smile as she helped disentangle my skirts from the curtain. Then she saw my trembling hands and her expression changed to one of concern. 'You look terrible pale, Miss Nora. Are you sickening for something?'

'No ... no, Millie. I'm fine ... really. I ... just saw ...' My gaze shifted to the moonlit lawn.

Millie's eyes widened, all traces of merriment gone. 'What did you see, miss?' she asked gravely.

'Th-that – boy,' I murmured. But as I pointed out into the darkness, I realised the boy was no longer there. I doubted myself suddenly. Perhaps there had been no boy? Merely a trick of the moonlight? Or ...

I turned to Millie and knew in an instant that I had not been mistaken. Her face was ashen. 'D-d-did you see him too, Millie?' I asked.

She shook her head most fervently. 'No, miss. You must never look at that boy!' she whispered urgently. 'Mrs Bell says he's one of the *Sluagh*...'

'What are the *sloo*?' I asked, speaking the word how she said it.

'The Sluagh are demons that come by night, searching for souls – that Sluagh boy can curse you with just one glance, miss!' Millie shivered.

I didn't tell her that I had looked into the boy's eyes. Nor of the fury I had seen in him.

But now I sit here in my chamber, questions and fears spinning webs in my mind. Is that boy really a demon? A Sluagh boy? Had he come to take my soul? Have I fallen under his curse? He did point at me with such anger in his eye … such vengeance …

An icy wind sweeps in through the gaps in the window frame, and I shudder.

Yet something troubles me – something doesn't fit. I saw that same boy crying, too. Can Sluagh cry?

I lift the edge of the curtain and peer into the blackness; a few flakes of snow are falling.

Another sleepless night beckons …

4th February 1839,
Hillsborough Castle

Dearest Diary,

Today nearly became the last day of my earthly life.

It all began with the snow which, having fallen fast all morning, by afternoon had transformed the gardens into a scene so white and perfect it made me doubt all the dark worries of the night.

Poor Cousin Caroline remained in bed, so Sancho once more was my only company. He made it quite clear that he did not wish to stay indoors, so we set off together for a walk. Sancho led the way through a veritable labyrinth of snowy paths and winter trees. But then, in the heart of a glade, Sancho charged off, chasing a squirrel, and vanished from sight. I tore after him but soon lost his trail in a fog which had suddenly risen.

I stumbled in circles, calling his name, and as twilight crept ever closer, I began to doubt my senses, thinking I glimpsed a pale face hiding in the snow-dappled shadows or that I heard the edges of a voice in the whispering wind …

At last, I entered a walled garden where I spied a building – a glass house with friendly smoke rising from its chimney. I ran towards it and went inside.

The heat hit me instantly; a furnace glowed at the far end of a long brick wall which was hot to the touch. The room was full of curious plants – low-lying and strangely shaped, like exploded stars, each with an extraordinary fruit sprouting forth.

'Pineapple?' I said in admiration, breathing in the sweet air. Only the wealthiest families kept an actual pineapple upon their mantelpiece – and then, only for parties. Yet here were so many … it made no sense. Before I arrived here, I heard talk of the lavish parties of Hillsborough Castle, but in reality this was not a place of merriment. I knelt to touch the strange, exotic fruit; its grand leaves perched like a crown upon a plump body of gold. King Pine!

The scrape of a shovel and the tumbling of coals – I turned to see a servant boy stoking the fiery mouth of the furnace. Relief surged through me as I ran towards him, explaining how I had become lost. The heat and smoke held me back and the furnace boy didn't even turn to face me, so busy was he feeding the coal. But he had heard me, it seemed, for he pulled down his cap and beckoned me to follow him out into the cool of the falling evening. I gazed at the pinkish sky; I had been warned not to be out past sundown.

'Which is the quickest way back to the castle, please?' I asked.

Still turned away, he beckoned and I followed – through the snowy orchard and along the shore of an icy lake. 'Are you sure this is the way?' I asked, for I saw no light ahead.

The furnace boy stopped walking. He swung around to face me and my heart froze in my chest. I knew him instantly! It was the boy I had seen in the night, the Sluagh boy, the boy so very feared and dreaded. His eyes locked on to mine, full of fury and vengeance.

I tried to scream but my throat was choked with terror. He stepped towards me and I backed away until my heels were right on the edge of the frozen lake. Snow was falling once again, whirling all around us in a white wind. In the breeze, something small and pale flew from the boy's pocket and landed at my feet.

I picked it up – a piece of paper, damp, fragile. It was a pencil sketch of a girl – around our age, with dark curls, freckles, smiling eyes. Cautiously, I held the picture out to the boy.

To my surprise, the boy's expression changed – a wave of pain and sorrow cutting through his rage. And I remembered then how I had seen him that first evening in the courtyard, weeping as though his heart was in a million pieces.

'Is this your sweetheart?' I asked.

The boy shook his head.

I tried again. 'Your … sister?'

'She died,' he said quietly, deep grief in his hollow eyes.

Snowflakes had settled on his dark lashes. 'I am sorry,' I whispered as I returned the picture to his hand. His skin was ice cold but I took his fingers in mine. 'I understand.' Some small comfort perhaps to know that he wasn't alone …

'I couldn't help her,' he said softly. 'I couldn't save her.'

'I'm sure you tried your best.'

The boy just closed his eyes. Tears rolled like beads of ice down his cheeks.

Then his eyes shot open – flashing once more with fury. 'I called for help!' he hissed. 'But nobody heard. There was a party. They were dancing and singing and celebrating.' He spat each word like it was poison. 'Nobody heard me …' His eyes were fire-bright with anger. 'Nobody came!'

And I realised then that the people of Hillsborough Castle were right to be afraid, but wrong for their reasoning. The boy was no demon, no soul-seeking Sluagh! He was simply a poor furnace boy who had lost his sister and whose grief was so deep he thought that only revenge would heal it. Perhaps I could help him find another solution …

A sudden bark interrupted us. Sancho! But before I could call his name, a rabbit came hurtling out of the bushes ... and behind it, Sancho charged straight on to the frozen lake. I shouted his name, but he was in the chase and paid me no heed.

The ice gave a tremendous creak and a splitting crack ... then it gave way entirely.

Poor Sancho slid, claws scrambling, yelping pitifully, and sank within the black waters.

Instincts surged in me, overtaking all sense, and I bounded forwards, ready to drag him to safety. With one foot upon the frozen lake, I felt an icy grip fasten on my wrist.

'Let me go!' I yelled to the boy. But he would not. His hold tightened. His touch so cold, it burned.

Sancho's paws were clawing at the crumbling ice, as he tried to climb out.

'Please!' I gasped, hearing the desperation in his barks. 'I must go to him!'

But the boy held me fast, his eyes boring into mine. 'I couldn't help her … I couldn't save her …' he whispered. 'But I can save you! If you walk upon the lake, you WILL die …'

Deep down, I knew the boy was right. 'But … Sancho!' I sobbed. His grey head was sinking under. He was weakening – he needed a way out of the water, quickly.

I peered all around in desperation, then, with my free hand, I pointed at a fallen branch. The boy nodded, understanding immediately. Together, we flung the branch on to the ice.

Sancho, wise at last, placed his paws on it and we dragged his wet body from the water. Then he staggered, shivering, to my side.

I tore off my coat and wrapped it around him, rubbing him warm, soothing him with kind words. 'We must hurry home,' I gasped, for the cold was biting. I turned to the boy to thank him, but he had vanished entirely.

I blinked in confusion. Then I realised he had probably dashed back to the pinery to stoke the furnace before the temperature dropped and all the precious pineapples shrivelled with frost.

Sancho gave a bark and tugged at my skirts, and we ran back to the castle where the lamps had been lit and the windows shone golden.

I flung myself through the doors and there, pacing in the entrance hall, was Cousin Caroline. I was so astonished to meet her at last, yet also concerned, for her cheeks were deathly pale and wet with tears.

'Oh Nora!' she declared, wiping her eyes. 'I am so relieved. I was quite beside myself with worry that something dreadful had become of you, just like—' and she stopped herself mid-sentence, as though she were about to unlock a truth to which she preferred to guard the key.

I was about to explain all that had happened but Cousin Caroline allowed me no time and instead sent me straight up to bathe and change before supper.

And this is where I am writing now, warm and clean once more. But my mind turns over and over on one question, so large it overshadows everything: what might have become of me were it not for that boy?

8th February 1839
Hillsborough Castle

Dearest Diary,

I write to you from my sickbed with Sancho snoozing upon my feet. Unsurprisingly, both of us have caught a chill after what Mrs Bell calls our 'little escapade'. Yet, despite my ill health, the mood here at Hillsborough Castle seems to be improving. Millie has informed me cheerily that there have been no sightings of the Sluagh boy for several nights – the servants are convinced he has passed on to a better place. I had not the heart to tell her that her superstitious fears had been unfounded – now that they are calmed, what would be the point?

And dear Cousin Caroline is quite transformed – so much so that I scarce recognise her! It feels as though she, too, has begun to thaw. I daresay, my long-held hopes of a splendid friendship with her no longer seem so very far away.

I do think a great deal about the furnace boy, hearing his words over and over in my head: *I couldn't save her ... but I can save you.* As soon as my health allows, I shall visit the pinery to thank him properly.

11th February 1839
Hillsborough Castle

Oh, Diary!

It has been the strangest of days. I finally was well enough to walk with Sancho to the pinery, but as soon as I entered the walled garden I saw that all was changed: no smoke rose from the chimney of the glass house and its windows were feathered with frost. I rushed forwards and flung open the doors, dreading what I would find.

The pinery was quite empty; the earth that just last week had flourished with green leaves and golden pineapples was now bare and frozen hard as rock. Nothing grew here. The furnace itself was cold, only old ash in the grate.

I explored further and found a rough jacket, as if forgotten. Distractedly, I ran my hand over it and something rustled in the pocket. Reaching in I drew out a piece of paper. It was the sketch the boy had shown me of his poor, lost sister. But now where was he? I turned over the sketch and saw written words that stilled my very heart with their strangeness.

Farewell, and thank you.

I charged all the way back to the castle – we had to call out a search for the boy and make sure he was all right.

I ran to the library, hoping to find Cousin Caroline, but the room was empty. Turning to leave, my eyes caught upon that same old newspaper, now lying open on the table. I read the headline with a gasp:

DOUBLE TRAGEDY STRIKES AT HILLSBOROUGH CASTLE

On 4 October 1837 a terrible accident occurred in the grounds of Hillsborough Castle, home of the Earl of Hillsborough and his new wife, Lady Caroline.

Kathleen Byrne, age 12, sadly drowned in the lake. The girl's brother, Jeremiah Byrne, 13, furnace boy at the famous Hillsborough pinery, had attempted to rescue his sister, but tragically lost his life. Due to the lavish celebration that had been taking place at the time, the children's cries had not been heard. The entire Hillsborough household is said to be distraught.

Tears fell down my cheeks.

Finally, I understood everything. Poor Jeremiah – even in death he had been plagued with guilt about his sister's drowning, so he had lingered beyond his natural time. All who lived here had felt his tragic presence ... perhaps they too felt guilty.

All Jeremiah really wanted was to save his sister, but what was done could never be undone, so instead his restless ghost sought revenge. But revenge helps no one. Once again, I heard his words in my mind: *I couldn't save her ... but I can save you.*

The boy who saved my life had already lost his own. And perhaps, in saving me, he'd found peace at last.

Now I gaze out over the frost-white gardens, the moon is rising full and bright.

'Farewell, and thank you,' I whisper.

And all is quiet. All is still.

The Tower Of London

RUN, RABBIT, RUN

By Catherine Johnson

E ddie Cartwright walked out of the tailor's shop on Hassel Street, feeling like he'd grown another four inches. He took a moment to check his reflection in the shop window. He looked proper smart, more of a man than a boy. He could wear it tomorrow at the memorial service for Dad's old regiment, at the Tower of London. He thought back to the invitation propped up in pride of place on the mantelpiece at the flat.

Memorial Service
at
THE TOWER OF LONDON
to honour the
memory of

Yes, Eddie thought to himself. He'd look the cat's whiskers in his new suit – he'd do his dad proud.

His thoughts were interrupted as Uncle Tony came out of the shop behind him. 'Looking sharp!' He whistled. 'You are the spit of your dad!'

'Thanks, Uncle Tony,' Eddie said. He would have liked to ask Tony more about Dad, but he knew Tony always thought his dad was a sap for joining up.

Tony laughed. 'Think of it as my early birthday present to you.'

Eddie took another look. Those lapels! And two vents. He knew Tony had some kind of deal with the tailor, but even so, it must have cost a bomb. More than a year's worth of Eddie's Saturday job money. Uncle Tony paused at a newspaper stand, and as Eddie glanced over, a headline screamed out at him in black letters bigger than his hand.

MAN SHOT DEAD IN EAST END

As Tony strode ahead, Eddie walked fast to catch up.

'Just don't tell your mother where you got the suit,' Tony called over his shoulder as Eddie followed him across Commercial Road. 'You know what she thinks of me. And your grandad for that matter.'

Eddie said nothing. Mum hated Uncle Tony, and Grandad said that even though Tony was his youngest, he was a wrong 'un.

'I promised your dad I'd look after you,' Tony said. 'And that's exactly what I'm going to do. Not long till you've finished with school, eh?'

'One more year,' Eddie said, adjusting his cuff. 'Then I'll be 15 and can get a real job.'

'Well, when it comes to work, you leave that to me,' Tony said. 'We Cartwrights deserve the best.'

Eddie walked a little taller. He stopped at the corner to watch Tony unlock his car.

'Thanks again, Uncle Tony.'

Tony leaned on the roof of the car. 'You look a million dollars, Eddie boy.' He paused, then pointed straight at Eddie. 'You know, there is something you can do for me. Well, for us.'

Eddie felt a knot tighten in his stomach. He knew who the 'us' was. Tony's Guvnor. Grandad said he was scum, but everyone knew the Guvnor ran the East End of London. People didn't stand in the Guvnor's way or they'd get cut down. As Eddie thought about this, the suit suddenly weighed a little heavy. Tony spotted his unease and came closer, putting an arm around Eddie's shoulder.

'Listen, Eddie. This could make you, son. Show the Guvnor who you are, what you're made of …'

Eddie thought of Mum and Grandad. If he worked with Uncle Tony and got himself a car, he could drive Grandad around, he could take Mum down the shops ...

Eddie nodded. Made his voice sound like the man he wanted to be. 'Course.'

'Smart boy.' Uncle Tony hugged him hard.

***

Later that afternoon, Eddie walked back to the flats with the bag Tony had given him. He wasn't going to tell anyone about this, not even Ray or Malcolm. He hadn't looked inside. Couldn't. It was a heavy canvas tool bag, and if he kept it tight closed, Eddie told himself it wouldn't matter what was in it – he was only looking after it for a couple of weeks.

He sped up, wanting to get home as soon as possible. This really could be his ticket to the big time, not breaking his back for years like Grandad. Nice suits, cars ... respect. And after all, what was he doing that was so terrible? Just looking after something for Tony's boss, that's all.

He stepped across the road and dodged through the traffic.

Suddenly, he heard a shout. 'Ed?! Eddie!' He clutched the bag tight, on high alert.

Another shout, 'Eddie!' Eddie eventually looked up to see that it was only Ray from school.

'Look at you!' Ray whistled. 'Cor! That a suit new?'

'As it goes, mate.' Eddie shifted the bag and kept walking towards the flats and home, and Ray fell into step. Eddie wished he would go.

Ray kicked at a stone. 'You coming to youth club later?'

Eddie indicated his suit with his free arm. 'Not tonight. Not in this!'

'Well, fancy a kick-about tomorrow?'

'I'm taking Grandad to the Tower of London, ain't I?'

Ray mimed a knife across his neck, then made a face. 'Watch your head, Ed!'

'Don't be daft. They don't kill people at the Tower anymore. Not for hundreds of years.'

Ray narrowed his eyes. 'My dad said the last person who was killed there was in the war.' He mimed a rifle, pointed it at Eddie. 'German spy.' Ray said. He let the shot go. 'See you tomorrow!' Ray called and Eddie watched him go.

Eddie felt less jittery when he reached the staircase that led to home and he took the stairs two at a time before reaching his front door.

He crossed his fingers and hoped Mum wasn't in.

Inside, he could hear Grandad whistling one of those old war tunes. *Run, Rabbit, Run, Rabbit ...* Eddie opened the door as quietly as he could and went into his bedroom.

He looked around – where to put the bag? What if Mum or Grandad found it? He swallowed hard. Perhaps there was nothing bad in the bag, after all. But who was he kidding? Eddie could feel something hard and metal through the canvas.

It was a gun.

Before he could argue himself out of it, he opened his drawer, made a space at the back and shoved the bag in. He closed his eyes, remembered the newspaper headline, heard his grandad whistling, and slammed the draw shut.

'Eddie?' Grandad called from the hall.

'Coming, Grandad!' he called back, trying to keep his voice steady.

Eddie left the bedroom and saw Grandad, pale as a sheet, leaning against the wall as if to stop himself from falling.

'Grandad?' He stepped towards the old man, feeling strangely cold as if he was suddenly moving through icy water. Grandad groaned. Eddie was suddenly terrified – was the old man on his way out?

Grandad's eyes were wide, watery.

'Ted? Teddy! Thank Gawd you're home, son …'

Eddie shook his head but couldn't speak. He wasn't Ted. Ted was his dad.

Grandad folded Eddie into a hug just as Mum appeared through the front door, shopping bags in each hand.

'Mo!' Grandad said to her. 'It's Ted. He's back.'

**

Later, after Grandad had gone to bed, Mum and Eddie sat in the front room. The picture of Eddie's dad, smart in his uniform and forage cap, smiled down from the mantelpiece, alongside the invitation to the Tower of London.

'Your grandad said he sees him sometimes … your dad.' Mum let out a long sigh. 'My Ted.'

'Do you reckon he's gone doolally?'

'No, love! He just misses him,' Mum said. 'And this service, for Dad's regiment, it's bringing everything back.'

Eddie said nothing. He'd only been two years old when Dad died. Eddie wished he had some memories of him.

'I don't know why your grandad even wants to go to the Tower tomorrow, it'll only make everything worse…'

Eddie frowned. 'Why? What happened at the Tower of London?'

'Not now, Eddie.' Mum sniffed a little, then looked up at Eddie. 'You look more like your father every bloody day,' she said. 'Especially all grown-up in that suit. Where did you get it from, anyway?'

Eddie stayed silent, looking down at his feet. Mum was suddenly furious.

'If that's from Tony, then you're to take it back tomorrow. He's trouble.' Mum put her hands on Eddie's arm. 'Listen to me, Eddie Cartwright. You stay away from him. You get your leaver's certificate next year and then a decent job.'

Eddie pulled away. 'What, like Grandad? In the fish market or the print shop?'

'Nothing wrong with that …'

Eddie stood up. 'You just want me to rub along like you. Little job, little life! That's not what Dad would have wanted for me!' Eddie saw the look on Mum's face, and for a split second he wished he could take his words back.

'Don't you bring your father into this!' Mum said, her voice rising. 'He was a good man! A decent man! Everything Tony isn't!'

Eddie stormed out to his bedroom. Grandad was going nuts, and Mum wanted him here under her thumb. But Tony was offering something better. He glanced at the drawer, picturing what he knew was hiding there, and felt a little sick. But he'd promised Tony he'd keep it safe, and if he was going to make something of himself he would need to keep his promise.

***

The next day, Eddie and Grandad caught the bus from Stepney Green, getting off at Tower Hill.

'Don't tell your mother, but I swear I've seen Ted more than once,' Grandad said as they walked towards the memorial service together. 'And for a moment there, you in that whistle suit …' Grandad shook his head. 'Oh, I miss him. Your mum misses him, too. She only wants the best for you, you know.'

Eddie wanted to say that Tony wanted better for him too, but he kept his mouth shut. A bell rang the hour for ten o'clock as Eddie led Grandad through the arch into the Tower of London.

Outside the chapel, a knot of men in uniform were talking. Eddie saw his Grandad's step grow lighter. 'Some of them served with your dad, when he was stationed here.'

Eddie only knew bits and pieces about his dad. Scots Guards, evacuated at Dunkirk, stationed in the Tower. But he was certain something had happened here, something nobody would talk to him about. According to Tony, Dad hadn't been the same after his time at the Tower.

Dad ended up in hospital – Tony said it was a 'nuthouse' – and died of tuberculosis.

'Grandad?' Eddie asked. 'What happened to Dad in the war?'

'All you need to know is that your father was a bloody hero,' Grandad said, before walking off, his stick raised in greeting.

Eddie looked round. The Tower of London was ancient, grey and forbidding. It seemed to have risen out of the ground from another time. It was mad, he thought, that this castle, this fortress, could just be here in the middle of the city. Like something out of a film.

Eddie put his hands in his pockets and leant against a wall. If Mum and Grandad wouldn't talk to him about Dad, maybe there was someone here who would.

As he looked around, he saw a man in uniform march away from the chapel and through a small archway. Eddie did a double take. *Dad?*

Eddie shook his head and laughed to himself under his breath. Maybe he was going doolally, too.

But he couldn't shake the weird feeling he'd got when he saw the soldier. Perhaps he'd go after him, just to prove to himself that he wasn't going mad.

He went in the direction the soldier had walked and, as he rounded a corner, he saw him again – marching, arms swinging, down what looked like an ordinary street; small, terraced houses built into the outer wall of the Tower, front doors, windows with curtains. The man started whistling. *Run, rabbit, run, rabbit, run, run, run ...*

Eddie had almost caught him up. He did look

RUN, RABBIT, RUN

uncannily like Dad – the shape of the head, the slope of the shoulders. Maybe this was the bloke Grandad had seen around.

Eddie called out. 'Scuse me!' He tried again, louder. 'Mister! Hang on!'

The soldier stopped. As he turned, Eddie suddenly felt like a hundred cold knives were slicing through him. The pale blue eyes staring into his own felt like looking in the mirror. But the man's skin was as grey as death.

'Dad?' Eddie whispered. It couldn't be. And yet, Eddie felt inexplicably drawn towards him.

In his haste to catch up with him, he suddenly tripped. His first thought was the suit – he didn't want to ruin it! He felt sick and dizzy all of a sudden, even though he hadn't hit the ground. And now the soldier seemed to have vanished altogether. Eddie blinked. Where had he gone? How was that even possible?

Eddie stood up and shook his head. Looked round at the street. Was the light different? The windows of the houses certainly were. Gone were the coloured curtains, just criss-crossed black tape on the windows in their place. As Eddie went to brush himself down, he realised he wasn't wearing the suit anymore.

He was head to toe in khaki. Black boots on his

feet, and he could feel a cap on his head – just like the one the soldier had been wearing.

Suddenly, someone shouted. 'Cartwright!' His name. He spun round. 'Private Cartwright!' The voice bellowed again.

The man shouting was in uniform, too. He was loud and fierce. 'With me! Now! Quick, march!'

Eddie started marching. How did he even know how to march? He followed the officer along the street, the great turrets of the White Tower shading out the sky. He tried to ask what he was doing, where they were going, but his mouth wouldn't work. While his arms swung and his feet stomped, any control he'd had over himself evaporated. He wanted to scream, to shout, to stop, but he just kept marching and swinging his arms in time with the other soldier. A puppet.

The man stopped, swivelled round. His face was so close that Eddie could see the flecks of spittle on his moustache. Eddie felt trapped inside this body, this person ... this *spirit*. Shut in, terrified.

Overhead, a scream of fighter planes blotted out the officer's shouting, as four Spitfires flew past. *What!* Eddie thought. *It can't be. Not in 1961.*

'In here, Cartwright! NOW!' yelled the officer. And Eddie found himself marching towards a courtyard at the outer wall of the Tower. He felt a heavy

sensation in his hands. He looked down and, although he didn't remember being given it, there was a gun. A rifle. As if in a trance, he shifted it on to his shoulder, and as he did so he spotted seven other soldiers, dressed identically to him – sombre, quiet – lining up alongside him. Where was he? And then he spotted him – tied to a chair. A man.

Eddie had never seen someone visibly shaking as this man was. He was vibrating –like a leaf, or a puppy waiting for the boot – with a face as pale as paper, his hair parted severely above his left eye. There was a white square, a handkerchief, pinned over his left breast pocket, and it moved as he shook. Like a tiny flag of surrender.

Then the man looked up, straight into Eddie's eyes, and Eddie could not look away. The rifle in his hands seemed to weigh a ton.

'Shoulder arms!' came the shout. Eddie felt the weight of the gun shift. He was holding it, ready to fire. He'd never held a gun; how did he know this stuff?

'Ready to fire?!' He felt his guts churning. Eddie willed the fellow to look away, but he did not – his stare coursing through Eddie's skin.

Eddie wanted to run, to scream, but his feet were welded to the spot.

'Shoot straight,' the man in the chair said quietly,

his voice trembling.

'Take aim!' Somehow Eddie found himself squinting down the sights, straight at the white hanky. The men around him did the same. They were there to kill him – eight men shooting one man. One man tied to a chair, like an animal in a trap. A mouse. A rabbit ...

Somewhere over the wall, in the outside world beyond the Tower, someone was whistling. *Run, rabbit, run, rabbit, run, run, run ...*

Eddie felt the trigger under his finger. If he pulled it, that man was dead. Time slowed, and although his body was not his own, his mind suddenly whirred to his life at home – Mum, Grandad ... the brooding hulk of metal nestled at the back of his drawer. Eddie felt sick. He felt the pressure of the trigger once again and the yell, long and drawn out as if he was listening under water – FIRE! A volley of gunshots filled his brain, louder than any firework, loud enough that it consumed his entire head. Skull trying to break free of flesh. And then, *ringing, ringing, ringing*. The smell of cordite, of gunpowder, as the bullets loosed.

Eddie's finger hadn't moved. Inside whatever this puppet, made of skin and bone, was, he couldn't move. He couldn't do it. Kill a man like this. A man sat there, staring at him.

As time slowed further, Eddie could see the bullets flying towards the man and red flowers blooming on the hanky on his chest. The smell of blood, sharp and iron. The man in the chair smiled. And Eddie screamed, his mind conjuring up the image of the newspaper stand – could that have only been yesterday?

MAN SHOT DEAD IN EAST END

Then the officer was shaking Eddie and the man tied to the chair had slumped sideways. Dead.

Eddie was still screaming when he realised it was Grandad shaking him, outside the chapel. The other men looked over, embarrassed for him. But Eddie was too relieved to find himself back in sole charge of his arms, legs and body to care.

'Eddie? You all right?'

'I saw Dad!' Eddie gasped, his heart still hammering and his hands shaking. Grandad sat him down on a bench.

'Stands to reason, here of all places.' Grandad looked up at the Tower. 'Breathe easy, son. Tell me what happened.' The words tumbled out of Eddie – the firing squad, the dead man. The smell of the bullets and the blood. Dad had been part of … no. Yes! A firing squad.

'I had to pull the trigger and ... and ...' Eddie shook his head. 'I couldn't do it! *I* couldn't kill him? Or *Dad* couldn't. It was like I was a part of him, but he ... I ... couldn't do it. The man was German. He was just sat there ...' Eddie shut his eyes and heard the sound of the bullets all over again.

Grandad sighed. 'Ted said the firing squad did it for him,' he said, opening up at last. 'It's not like the enemy, in battle – not when a fellow's strapped up and not moving.'

'But he was a German!'

'Course.' Grandad shrugged. 'German spy. Name of Jakobs. Came down in a field somewhere, caught right away. But taking a life, even in war – it's not an easy thing.'

***

On the bus home, Eddie read Grandad's paper, about the man shot the day before yesterday. He was called Mr Freedman; he had two kids. The paper said it was the Guvnor's gang. Did Tony know about it? What if Tony had actually done it? Had shot Mr Freedman dead? Eddie shuddered. What would Tony do if he broke his promise? What would the Guvnor do?!

Eddie suddenly felt as cold as ice, the sound of bullets roaring back into his head.

'You all right, son?' Grandad said. Eddie forced a smile. He tried not to think about what would happen if he gave the gun back ... but he also didn't want to think about what might happen if he kept it.

Eddie didn't sleep a wink that night. Every time he shut his eyes he saw the man in the chair, heard the volley of gunfire. The smell of cordite and blood.

He was still awake when he heard Mum leave for work at seven. Then he got up, got dressed and slipped out of the house.

Heart pounding, he stopped at the foot of the steps and watched people going to work and to school, just like normal. He shifted the bag under his arm. It was heavier now, with the suit too. He had to take them back to Tony. He had to. What would happen after that, he couldn't be sure – but he'd cross that bridge when he came to it.

He felt the skin prickling on the back of his neck and he span round and looked up at the flat. Was that Grandad looking out? No, the figure at the window was wearing khaki. And an army cap. As Eddie watched, the figure at the window nodded, then – and Eddie knew he would remember it for the rest of his life – gave him a salute. And when Eddie nodded back, he swore his dad smiled.

KENSINGTON PALACE

THE DOLL'S HOUSE

By Jasmine Richards

I have no memories of the first time I visited the Queen at Osborne House. Perhaps I had been a babe in arms? I imagine it now. Being held to my mother's chest as she swept up the stone steps. Feeling her warmth beneath my cheek, the softness of her skin and the roughness of lace at her collar. But now she is gone. The thought sits heavy in my chest. My mother – Sarah Aina Forbes Bonetta – is dead.

Mother had spoken of Osborne House before, but her eyes had been wary, which seemed strange to me at the time. Mother had spent many summers in the royal residences of the Queen, playing with her children. Playing the dutiful god-daughter. She had been a lucky penny, brown and glitteringly bright, turning up in all corners of the kingdom.

On the long journey from Cheltenham Ladies' College to the Isle of Wight, I had imagined what Osborne House might look like – grand and overwhelming – and I had not been wrong. The carriage rolled down an impressive tree-lined avenue, past pale yellow stone façades and a large fountain surrounded by bronze dragons. A fortress of order, I thought, and wondered if it might barricade the grief straining to be free inside me. A beast I would not look in the eye.

As I stepped down from the carriage, a silent maid, her expression unreadable, curtsied before ushering me inside. My travelling cloak was suffocating in the sweltering heat, but nobody offered to take it from me. And I wasn't going to take it off myself. I, Victoria Matilda Davis, was not raised in a barn. I had been schooled in the art of etiquette by the college and I was a diligent student.

As I stepped into the maw of the Queen's home, I welcomed my cloak. It felt like a second skin. Protection. This gilded house had me quite agitated, scaring me even though I did not understand why.

I had not yet cried. I had wanted to on the voyage from the mainland. I'd wanted to howl and sob during the long hours, but something in me had locked tight. Could this fear piercing me be sadness, but by another name?

And then I saw her.

Queen Victoria sat in her great Burmese teak chair. Black fabric a billow of smoke around her. Black. The symbol of death and grief. And yet black was always love to me. The Queen did not stand as I entered. She merely beckoned me forwards with a small, gloved hand.

'My dear child.' Her voice was softer than I expected. 'Come.'

I curtsied, hesitated, then stepped closer. My feet felt so heavy. Clods of clay.

The Queen took my hands in hers. 'I am dreadfully sorry for your loss.' She studied me. 'Please know, your mother was very dear to me. Sweet, clever Sarah. A treasure taken too young.'

I swallowed, but my throat remained dry. *A treasure?* I wanted to say. *Taken?* And all I could hear was my father's voice, gruff with whispered fury as he argued with my mother. Papa, who was now so far away from me. He had said that our family needed to be more than obedient shadows. That we were not objects on a shelf. Nor animals in a menagerie for people to look upon with curiosity. Then my mother's voice. Angry, but lower and imperious. Her accent sharp like glass, saying that Papa could not possibly understand what it meant to be the godchild of a queen.

Her Majesty sighed, as if disappointed or irritated by my silence. 'She would want you to be strong, Tilly,' the Queen said. 'And you shall be. As she was. Sarah, the finest flower of the Empire.'

I flinched at that, and the Queen tapped my hand firmly – a reminder of what reactions were permissible and which were not. She was right. My mother had been a flower, but I am not sure she ever found soil for her roots. Not here, not there, not anywhere. And now she was gone.

'I have something for you,' the Queen continued. 'A remembrance of your mother. I think it will bring you great comfort.'

At these words, two servants appeared from the shadows with a whisper-soft tread that spoke of practice. They lifted a sheet of the finest Indian cotton from the table beside the Queen's chair and revealed – a doll's house. A perfect replica of a grand townhouse. Not some whimsical child's toy, but an imposing structure, standing tall with its flat roof and painted brick exterior. Something about it made me tense up. A delicate fanlight arched above the red-painted door, and there were four windows on the ground floor and six on the top floor.

Inside, miniature rooms were furnished with

the finest details – silk curtains, tiny gilt-framed paintings, even a miniature piano no bigger than my palm. And dolls stood unmoving in every room. Made of wood and painted white, they looked like porcelain. They had pink cheeks and carved smiles that were frozen in place. But there, in the centre of the parlour, was a doll that stood alone.

This one was brown, unpainted, with whorls that spoke of the age of the wood it was carved from. Unlike the others, the face was completely featureless. No identity gifted to it.

This doll was smaller than the others, its white dress swallowing its tiny form. It looked so lonely that I could not help but reach out to it. As my fingers touched the smooth wood, it thrummed and an intense feeling of familiarity, speared me. It left me with a quiet panic that I could not explain. I snatched my hand away.

'This doll's house belonged to me as a child before I gave it to Sarah,' the Queen said. 'It was built at Kensington Palace by my servants. Those dear hearts took scraps of wallpaper from the palace to adorn miniature walls and gathered up old fabric to make tiny curtains.'

The Queen rose from her chair and approached the table, her fingers brushing the roof of the doll's house. 'Such an act of adoration from them … or perhaps pity. To build a real home from the bones of that wretched palace.'

I frowned, wondering what she meant by pity, and why she called Kensington Palace 'wretched'.

The Queen lingered, staring into the parlour. 'The dolls were my only friends, Tilly. I would play with them for hours on the yellow carpet. In that miniature world, no one monitored my manners or corrected my posture. No one dictated where I could go, what I could say. I was not watched.'

She glanced at me then, her eyes furious. 'Because I was *always* watched. The governess. My mother. Sir John. I could not descend a staircase without permission. There were rules for everything. Sir John's system.' Her voice became faint. 'But here …' She stroked the roof with one finger. 'Here, the rules did not follow me.'

I could tell the Queen was quite lost to her memories now, and I studied the curve of her cheek and the beak of her nose. She looked haunted.

She turned to me. 'Your mother was delighted when I gave this doll's house to her. She loved playing with it as a child.'

She did not, I thought. Mother never spoke of dolls. Not once. She spoke of books, music, the places we would travel to. Of how to keep one's chin tilted high and one's voice steady. But dolls? Never.

When I was younger and the nursery governess offered me little dolls wrapped in lace and bows, my mother would smile tightly and steer me towards a puzzle box instead. Or encourage me to learn a tune by ear. She always found a different game. A different way. I realised that now.

'You will stay here at Osborne House for a while, as was arranged before we both received this terrible news,' the Queen said, looking at me directly. 'We shall arrange for your return to Cheltenham when term starts again. But for now, you must rest.'

I knew a dismissal when I heard one. I curtsied again, the weight of grief keeping me down far longer than it should have. I let the maid lead me to my room. The doll's house followed – carried by those that came from the shadows.

I ate in my room and the doll's house sat in the far corner of the chamber, its tiny windows facing me like many unblinking eyes. It was Frankenstein's monster – stitched together of many parts. Watching me. I wanted to turn it to the wall, but refused to give in to foolish impulses.

Instead, I sat on the edge of my bed, running my fingers over the strip of cloth in my lap. The same fabric my mother had given me before I left for the college. It was a small scrap, no larger than a handkerchief, but I clung to it now. This fabric had travelled with my mother across continents and years. It had remained with her after the murder of her parents by a rival kingdom. After she was gifted to Queen Victoria. I wove the fabric between my fingers and made a knot of remembrance that pulled tight and made my skin protest.

I traced the cloth's frayed edge, and started to hum softly. An old melody that Mother would croon to me when I was sad. She said the words were right on the tip of her tongue, just out of reach. It would upset her, sometimes. All the things she had forgotten. All those things she had lost when she was brought across the sea by Captain Forbes.

My chest felt tight. That beast of grief was stirring inside me again. I lay my head on the pillow, feathers scratching my cheek through the material. The candle flickered beside me, and I watched it dance, hoping it would bring sleep. I wondered when news of mother's death would reach my father. There had been oceans between them. A quiet separation that we all knew of but did not mention.

The hush of the room crouched in the corners. Waiting. Then the faintest of whispers, thin as a cobweb, wrapping around the silence. I lay still on the pillow. Listening. Wood creaking now as well, expanding, stretching. As if something inside the room was waking. I sat up, my pulse a drum. The candle scarcely lit the room. My eyes finally found the far side of the chamber. The doll's house. Its little red door was slightly ajar.

Had it been open before?

Had it?

Had it?

The question was a new drumbeat going through me.

I slid out of bed, my feet slapping against the cold wooden floor as I crossed the room. My breath was loud and uneven. But I needed to check on her. The little brown doll.

Loss rolled over me like a wave as I looked into the parlour. The doll was not there. She had been sitting in the house when I last checked. Now, she was gone. In the gloom, I searched, my movements frantic. And then I saw her on the ground, lying on her side, arms outstretched.

My skin prickled into gooseflesh. I must have knocked her over earlier. Or perhaps the maid, when she brought in my bags. Yes. That was it. I reached down, and gently lifted her.

The doll thrummed in my hand like before, and as I looked at the blank space where there should be a painted face, I saw the shadow of long lashes. The curve of full lips. And as I placed her back in the parlour, I was once again struck by how lonely she looked. The other dolls frozen in their neat domestic poses seemed at home. But my doll … she looked trapped, and it was suddenly unbearable to witness. I turned away, went back to my bed and blew out the candle.

And in the darkness, I fell asleep thinking of a wooden face that shared the same smile as my mother.

And at midnight, I dreamed of the *tip-tap, tip-tap* of tiny footsteps walking on wood.

***

The next two days were a trickle of sand through fingers. In the day, I would sit with a book in my lap, pages unturned. The words always swam away just beyond reach. Bergamot-scented tea would cool in porcelain cups next to me. I dared not pick up the fragile teacups as the urge to crush them and scald my hand just to feel something was too strong.

Often, I imagined I could hear my mother's laugh in the low gust of the summer wind through a window and I would bite back a sob. At night, I longed to sleep but slumber was an apparition that did not visit readily. The second night, as I tossed in my sheets, I sat up with a sharp certainty that someone had whispered my name.

The candle beside was a ruined stump with a tiny flame. Across the room, the doll's house sat with its door open again, just as I had found it before. The brown doll had moved. She now stood beside the window of the miniature parlour, her head turned to face me in my bed. I did not remember placing her there.

In the morning, I told myself it must have been the maid. Or perhaps I had done it in my sleep. I dreaded the next night and was right to do so. I awoke from my half-dream to find the doll's house door was open again, although I had been sure to close it before getting into bed. This time, all the dolls stood at each of the windows. Their gazes stared downwards and I found the brown doll lying, not in the doll's house, but directly beneath the table where it stood. Her blank face was turned in my direction. It was as if she had tried to reach me and failed.

My stomach lurched. Perhaps she was trying to escape, this little doll swathed in white, but I knew I could not save her. I did not even know if I could save myself. Mother was gone and that beast of grief would consume me soon, I was sure. I placed the doll back in the house.

I could bear it no longer. I had to get the doll's house out of my room. Even the little brown doll. It did not matter that it was a gift from the Queen. I could feel its presence filling the room, pressing at my skin, boring a hole in my head. I lifted the doll's house off the table, gripping its sides. I just needed to get it to the door. It was weighty, but it was manageable. I shuffled forwards and suddenly it was so much heavier than it should have been.

I staggered under its weight. Was the doll's house resisting? My palms began to sweat as the wood of the structure heated up. Then my knees buckled and the base of the doll's house smashed down on the floor. What would the Queen say? Had I broken her treasured doll's house? I hated myself for caring because I knew it was a rancid thing.

I peered down at it and saw that it was not broken but something had loosened near the base. I frowned, feeling around the edge of the doll's house, and then a small compartment slid open. Inside was a tiny leather-bound journal. I pulled it out carefully, my fingers tingling.

The Doll's House

The leather was soft with age, the corners worn, the pages delicate but intact. As I turned it over, my breath caught.

Written in delicate cursive on the first page:

Sarah Aina Forbes Bonetta

I stared at my mother's name, a lump forming in my throat.

My hands shook as I turned the pages, my eyes racing over the words.

* * *

17th March 1855

I arrived at Kensington Palace today. It is cold, even though fires burn in the grate.

It was strange to visit the Queen here – she does not like this place, I think. She seems so stiff here. She looks over her shoulder as if expecting someone to be there.

The Queen had a gift for me. It was a doll's house. She said that she had played with it as a child. That it brought her comfort. Her eyes do not speak of comfort though, more of secrets.

The Queen's face was strange as she spoke of her

childhood at Kensington Palace. Her hands fidgeted in her lap. I had heard the rumours, of course. That as a child Victoria had been a prisoner in this palace. This place does not feel like a home. It feels like a place where you forget how to breathe.

I dare not tell her that something about this doll's house makes my stomach roil.

19th March 1855

I hate the doll's house. I wake to find its door open. The dolls do not remain where I carefully place them. They move when my gaze slides away.

The voices of the doll's house whisper to me.

I feel watched and I cannot untether the feeling that something is inside it. Something malicious. Waiting.

21st March 1855

Last night, I dreamed I was inside the doll's house. The walls pressed in. And it felt like the loneliness that often creeps over me when my mind is too still.

The elderly housemaid told me some more about the wicked regime she called the Kensington System today, and its architect, Sir John Conroy.

She spoke of a lonely little girl who would one day

be Queen and how that little girl was observed at all times. Never left alone – not even to walk down the stairs by herself. She was forbidden from playing with other children and forced to rely on Sir John for everything. A master of manipulation and persuasion. And no one stopped it. But they gave her a doll's house made of the fragments from Kensington Palace and told the child queen to smile.

I think I understand now – why she gave me this doll's house, even if she does not see the echo.

I was told how the Queen would have terrible rages as a child.

I feel rage too, sometimes.

I think it is because I remember things but never speak of them.

I remember my parents. I remember their murder. I remember the long journey across the sea. I remember my name – Aina – though no one calls me that any more. I write it down so I don't forget.

There is talk of sending me to Freetown, across the vast water. I long for it. I fear it. Mostly, I feel … in between. Like I do not belong here in England or there in Sierra Leone.

And when I sit near the doll's house, that feeling deepens. I think it remembers things, too. I think it holds on to pain.

And it holds on to it very tightly.

22nd March 1855

Today a new doll arrived in the doll's house. A brown wooden one. Its face is completely blank.

Not a single person in the palace can tell me where it has come from.

I made a white dress for it. Like the one I wear. I whisper my name in her ear and place her in the parlour of the doll's house.

The other dolls do not look at her. I think they are waiting for her to forget who she is.

Just as I have been made to forget.

This doll's house is not comfort.

It is a gaol built from scraps of Kensington Palace – wallpaper, curtains, pieces of another girl's prison. And now it is mine.

The doll's house is too full of a sorrow twisted into spite to be a safe place. But I do nothing. I leave the unpainted doll where it is.

And I wait.

And I wait.

* * *

I slammed the journal shut, my breath shuddering. Mother had been afraid of the doll's house, too.

I sit with that truth and do not know if it is for

minutes or hours.

I looked at the doll's house again, feeling a new resolve. Instead of trying to lift it, I pushed it across the floor. It made a screeching sound as I dragged it across the wooden boards and I thought my ears might bleed. I opened the door to my bedroom and forced the doll's house out into the empty corridor. I slammed the door shut and placed my forehead to the wooden panel, hoping I might hear footsteps soon and that someone would take the doll's house away.

It was done. I had got rid of it.

I turned.

I froze.

The doll's house was back in my room! Exactly where it had been before, on the table. The horrid truth of it all came to me. This doll's house was not haunted. It hunted. It hunted out pain. Just like my mother's pain. Just like the young Queen's. I had enough pain and grief to drown in. Now it hunted me.

* * *

I requested an audience with Queen Victoria, and she met me in the sitting room, her expression unreadable.

'Well, my dear,' she said, setting down a letter

she had been reading. 'What is it?'

I hesitated, plucking at my mother's strip of cloth that I had wrapped around my wrist. It lent me strength. 'The doll's house,' I said. 'It is ... evil.'

The Queen's eyebrows lifted slightly.

'It moves – it ...' I faltered, but I had come too far to stop now. 'I found my mother's journal. She was afraid of it, Your Majesty. She wrote that it was watching her. She wrote about hearing whispers.'

Something flickered in the Queen's expression. A flash of memory, perhaps?

'It holds something,' I continued before my courage could flee. 'Grief. Pain. My mother's loneliness – your own as well, I think. Because of your childhood and the Kensington System. It is all trapped inside it.'

The Queen's mouth pressed into a thin line. 'That is quite enough.'

'No, it is not,' I said and my voice sounded firm and true. 'The past is not dead. It lingers. It haunts. You speak of my mother as a flower, but do you realise how those roots were severed? She was a child, taken from her home, given a new name, a new life she never asked for. And this doll's house ...' I took a breath. 'This doll's house is a reminder of that.'

Queen Victoria rose from her chair. 'You are

distraught,' she said. 'You are ungrateful. Grief can play cruel tricks on the mind, Victoria Matilda.'

The Queen's voice lingered on the name Victoria. The name that had been given to me when I was presented to her by my mother. When I was given the title of godchild to the Queen.

'I am not mistaken,' I began.

'Go to your room and rest. And take that rag from your wrist. It is unseemly. Your mother used to have one just like it.'

I opened my mouth to argue, but a footman appeared in the doorway. The audience was over.

***

Back in my room, the doll's house was waiting for me. I would destroy it. Smash it to pieces. I knew I would be lost if I didn't. And the doll's house knew what was in my mind. The air changed. The candle beside my bed flickered violently, and a stale gust of wind swept through the room. I staggered backwards, my breath coming sharp and shallow now. A whisper began, rising from the doll's house. So many voices, but I could not understand what they were saying. And then the doll's house door creaked open.

The room lurched around me. I gasped as the floor tilted beneath my feet. My arms flailed, and then there was darkness. When I opened my eyes, I was inside the doll's house. In the parlour. The walls stretched upwards, too tall. The furniture sat at wonky angles with sickly yellow candlelight flickering over their edges. The air was stale and soupy, making me gag, and I stumbled to my feet. I needed to leave this place.

I searched for the doorway, and that is when I saw her. The wooden doll who was no longer a doll. A real girl was curled in the corner of the parlour, trembling. Her hands buried in the depths of her frilly white dress. I knew who she was, even in her child form.

'Mama,' I said the word out loud and I could hear the longing in my voice.

Something moved in the doorway and I turned to see pale dolls, dozens of them, staring at me with flat, painted eyes. They jostled and pushed to get through the door, their grins too wide. They whispered something that I could not quite catch.

I ran to my mother's side. She needed to know she had someone with her in this place. Mother shuddered as I wrapped my arms around her, pulling her close. I took the strip of fabric from my wrist and tied it around hers.

'You are not alone,' I whispered fiercely. 'I see

The Doll's House

you, Mama.'

The whispering words from the dolls suddenly became a scream and I realised what they had been saying all along. 'Stay.'

'I love you, Aina,' I told Mother. 'You will always be loved. You will always be remembered. I will lay down roots for us.'

The walls around us cracked. The floor shifted and then buckled. Light, no, *sunlight* poured from the chasm that had opened up in the ground. The house was coming apart. I closed my eyes and held my mother. And she held me. I woke up on the floor of my bedroom, gasping for air, not sure how long I had been there.

The doll's house lay in ruins. Splintered wood and broken pieces were scattered around my room, but there was no sign of the pale dolls.

The brown doll rested in my hand, wrapped in the cloth of my mother. The doll no longer thrummed. It was as if something had been set free. I stumbled to my feet – I knew what I had to do.

I tucked the doll under my arm, gathered up the shattered doll's house and left the room. The estate grounds were silent as I made my way to the fountain at Osborne House.

One by one, I dropped the fragments into the

fountain's basin. These pieces of the doll's house made from Kensington Palace bobbed on the surface for a moment and then sank.

I heard a noise. The faintest hiss. Or a sigh, maybe. I looked up. On the other side of the fountain, was Queen Victoria. She said nothing, as the last fragment sank to the bottom of the fountain. She just stared at me, and I could see both relief and fury on her face.

I turned away first, but not before I saw that the Queen held one of those pale dolls in her hand.

I left Osborne House for the college that day. The brown wooden doll wrapped like a gift in my mother's cloth.

I knew at last that Aina was free.

HAMPTON COURT PALACE

THE EXECUTIONER

By Larry Hayes

'Do you believe in ghosts?' asked Mr Dobson, the Palace Deputy Manager.

My twin sister Harriet and I both shook our heads. We were in the so-called, 'Haunted Gallery' of Hampton Court Palace, receiving our safety briefing.

'Well, if they do exist, then this is where you'll see one. This spot is where most of the faintings happen,' he explained.

'Faintings?' Harriet didn't look impressed.

'Yes, right where you're standing. That exact spot is said to be the most haunted place in the whole of the British Isles. It's where Catherine Howard was caught by King Henry VIII's guards and taken to the Tower of London for execution.'

The Executioner

We all looked down at the floor. It was wooden, covered with an old rug. 'People say they feel dizzy, as if their brain's turning round in their skull. Then down they go.'

We obviously didn't look adequately awestruck because he added, 'Sometimes people do worse than faint.'

'Like what?' said Harriet, smiling. 'Fill their pants?'

I knew Harriet well enough to know that she was just trying to get a reaction.

'Sorry about her,' I said. 'She's just trying to shock you.'

To be fair, he didn't even blink. He just said, 'Thank you, Jack – just stay together and you'll be fine. But remember sometimes ghosts can, literally, scare you to death.'

He left soon after that, clearly worried enough by Harriet's attitude to add, 'Please don't muck about. This competition was all my idea, and if anything goes wrong, I'll take the flack.'

Thinking back, it wasn't much of a safety briefing. He finished with, 'If you're worried, shout. I'm just in the office across the courtyard.'

Which, given what happened next, was pathetically inadequate.

But I'm getting ahead of myself. I need to go back to the beginning and explain how we ended up in the Haunted Gallery of Hampton Court Palace in the first place.

It all started thanks to Harriet.

***

She was born 13 minutes before me, and so she thinks she's my older sister. And, like all older sisters, she thinks that's a big deal. Harriet is one of those kids who's absolutely brilliant at absolutely everything. Gymnastics, maths, she even got a haiku published in the local newspaper to help stop littering. She's that kind of a sister – brilliantly perfect, and perfectly brilliant all at the same time.

So, when Hampton Court Palace ran a competition (first prize, a 'Ghostbusting Sleepover' in the Haunted Gallery), Harriet, of course, went and won it.

'Complete the following in 500 words or less: *I'm not afraid to spend the night in Hampton Court Palace, the most haunted palace in Britain, because …*'

When she won, you'd have thought she'd podiumed at the Olympics. And I must admit, I was jealous as hell. A night in maybe the most haunted place in Britain? It would be epic. The ultimate chance to find out if ghosts are real.

I thought she'd pick one of her annoying friends

from school. But she didn't. She chose me, her brother. Our parents were all clucky about that, in a 'That's so kind, Harriet. It makes us so happy to see you two finally getting along,' kind of a way.

But I was immediately suspicious.

Because Harriet is perfect with a twist. She is also the meanest, most-vindictive-and-downright-evil, practical joker on the entire planet.

And she has a favourite victim.

Me.

She's been haunting my existence from since I can first remember. On our fourth birthday she let her hamster climb over my birthday cake. It left little brown gifts which were kind of funny until you learn that hamster poo sometimes has tapeworm eggs that can eat their way up into your brain. Dad had to chuck the whole thing in the bin.

Yes, you heard that right, my four-year-old twin sister tried to kill me with a brain worm.

At Christmas, she takes the chocolate out of my advent calendar the night before. She finds it funny, every day, for a month. Every year. Sometimes she swaps them for mud, and I've learned to just throw chocolates away if I find any.

And don't get me started on Halloween. She once made me think I'd wet the bed by hiding ice cubes in the duvet. She took a photo and showed it round school.

Evil.

There's no better word.

As we wriggled into our sleeping bags, the Sun hovering low above the big clock tower across the courtyard, I knew something was coming. Because Harriet doesn't do kind; she doesn't have a kind bone in her body.

There in the Gallery, struggling to get comfortable in my sleeping bag, all I could think about was one thing: something was coming. Harriet would only ever invite me along to something like this if she had a twenty-four-carat-gold trick up her sleeve.

The Executioner

You're probably wondering why I agreed to go along. Why anyone would go along to have the living daylights scared out of them. There's a simple answer. For once, I had the advantage. Because I had the element of surprise. I knew she was up to something. But what she didn't know was that I meant to get my revenge in first. For the first time in my life, I had a prank of my own. And it was an absolute doozy. The ultimate revenge for a lifetime of misery.

Harriet was going to learn the lesson of her life.

* * *

The Sun disappeared quickly and we were soon turning on camping lights. Even with three, the Gallery was full of shadows. The old paintings came alive in the dim light, the ancient faces looked down on us suspiciously. Heavy curtains ran along the outside wall and a sudden thought jabbed into my brain – someone could easily hide in there. Or something. A ghost maybe, or worse.

I'd have been happy to bend the rules and go exploring, but Harriet insisted we stay in the Gallery. More proof that she had something planned –

Harriet's never followed a rule in her life.

She lay there, propped up on one elbow, and began to read from her phone. She'd found a site describing the ghosts of Hampton Court and was eager to share the grisly details.

'Check this out,' she said, her face deathly white in the light of her phone. 'That's what it looks like.'

She turned the phone to show a blurry CCTV image of a courtyard. A tall, hooded figure stood in the doorway, its long, black cloak concealing everything but a white skeletal hand.

'Is that her? Catherine Howard?'

'Maybe,' Harriet replied with a wicked grin. 'Who knows? This Gallery has two ghosts.'

I looked into the shadows of the empty Gallery. 'What's the other one?' I said, trying to sound nervous. For my plan to work, Harriet had to believe I was my usual, clueless self.

'Her Executioner.' Harriet's smile revealed sharp teeth. 'Here's a picture, but it's just an artist's impression.'

She thrust the phone at my face and I had to lean back to focus on the image of a black-hooded figure. It held a massive, blood-dripping axe.

'He looks friendly.' I smiled, not having to try quite so hard to look worried.

'King Henry VIII had Catherine Howard executed with an axe after she was accused of being unfaithful. In contrast, Anne Boleyn was beheaded by a sword – a quicker and more precise method, likely chosen to show her a final act of mercy. Catherine, who Henry VIII regarded with far less affection, was not granted the same consideration.' Harriet continued to read. *'Some say he even dissolved Catherine's body in quicklime.'*

'Dissolved?' I said, suddenly not needing to pretend to be afraid.

'Yeah, *dissolved.*' Harriet turned back to her phone. She was enjoying this. *'It says, Hampton Court Palace was the first building in the UK to have CCTV installed because the security guards refused to spend the night there. Anyone stupid enough to spend a night in the Haunted Gallery will hear the Executioner's blade as it's dragged across the flagstones of the lower hall. Then the thump of the axe as it is heaved up each step of the stairway leading into the Haunted Gallery.'*

We looked at the far door, shadows were merging in the gloom, the Sun long since gone.

I somehow knew Harriet would make her move then. I guess after 14 years, I just know her that well.

Not even bothering to get out of her sleeping

bag, she struggled upright and, clutching the bag around her, clumsily hopped, two-footed, over to the far wall. She stood there, staring, her face never once leaving the bright screen of her phone.

'Jack,' she said softly, 'that Dobson guy was right. This is the spot where the guards catch her, by this painting of Saint George and the Dragon.'

'The fainting spot,' I mumbled quietly.

'The guards grab poor Catherine here.' Harriet reached out with her hand as if she were somehow re-enacting the event. 'And her ghost relives the misery of her capture and death each and every night. Over and over, for all eternity.'

Harriet's voice was comically Halloweenish by now, and I struggled not to smile. Because what Harriet didn't realise was that I knew all about the Executioner. And the story of Catherine Howard. I'd done my research; spent weeks plotting and scheming. And this was all fitting perfectly with my brilliant plan.

I forced my face into a fearful frown, ready to act increasingly anxious.

But then Harriet did something so ridiculous, so totally over the top, that I couldn't help but smile. Still swaddled in her sleeping bag, she swayed forwards, then back, uselessly reaching out a hand to steady herself.

The Executioner

And then she crumpled, smacking hard on to the wooden floor as she fell.

'Harriet?' I fought to get out my own bag and ran to her. She lay there, eyes closed, and I gave her a prod with my foot.

She didn't even twitch; she was out cold.

Or so she wanted me to believe.

But I knew better – I knew this all had to be part of some elaborate prank. Some vicious practical joke designed to leave me a blubbering wreck. I looked down at her, limply cocooned in her thick sleeping bag, and had to resist giving it a kick.

Now, you're probably wondering how I could be so certain. So convinced that this was just a trick. And I must admit, for a moment I doubted myself. Even with all the years of tricks and no treats. Looking down on her pale, blank face, she really did look unconscious. But then I heard a noise. The distant sound of metal grinding over stone, and I knew instantly that this had to part of Harriet's plan. The timing was just too perfect.

It was all so obvious. Creepy noises in the night? That was kid's stuff. I even knew how she was doing it, because I'd considered the idea myself:

hide a Bluetooth speaker somewhere when they're not looking, and hit play on your phone when you're ready to freak them out.

Back home, plotting, I'd even tested it out. But the sound was never quite realistic enough.

The noise came again, and I had to force myself not to smile. It was so obviously fake.

Which reminded me – I had my own trick to execute. A much better trick. And Harriet's pathetic fainting act had given me the perfect excuse to sneak out, just as I'd planned.

'Don't worry, Harriet. I'll get help.' I said, my voice cracking with fake concern. And running, I disappeared into the shadows of the Gallery.

It took seconds to reach the head of the stairs, but I stopped dead as soon as I did. The curved stairwell, overlooking the entrance hall below, had been stuffed with people when we'd arrived. Now there was just a big, empty void. The massive paintings that filled the far wall were now invisible in the dark. Even the giant windows, looking out at the black night, seemed to suck away the light.

But most of all, I felt the heavy silence. The noise from Harriet's speaker, the sound of metal on stone, or whatever it was supposed to be, had gone.

I felt myself shiver. The floor beneath my bare feet felt unnaturally cold and I had to force myself onwards, cursing for forgetting my head torch.

'Stick to the plan,' I muttered to myself. And stepping carefully towards the head of the stairs, I groped in the dark for the railing. I inched down those stairs, gripping the smooth metal banister, wary on the uneven stone steps. At the bottom, they fanned out into semicircles and I had to leave the banister behind, cautiously stepping in the dark until I finally reached the ground floor.

I could see the double doors on to the courtyard now. A light from beyond glowed dimly through their glass panels. And walking more confidently across the chequered flagstones, I found what I needed.

Two fire extinguishers stood in the corner. I'd noted them on the way in – and the larger one, marked WATER in big, bold caps, was exactly what I needed. I grabbed it, struggling with the weight.

A door banged somewhere above, the noise echoing down into the empty hall, and I stopped, frozen.

It had to be Harriet, surely. Making noises to spook me out. She'd obviously recovered from her 'collapse' and wasn't wasting time in putting her own plan into action. A sudden thought struck me – there were all sorts of doors leading out of the Haunted Gallery. What if Harriet was somehow sneaking round – ready to jump me from behind? With Harriet, anything was possible.

I pulled at the extinguisher with new determination. It was heavy, but I just had to drag it. The metal rumbled across the floor satisfyingly. *Like a dragged axe*, I thought to myself, grinding the extinguisher across the flagstones with a satisfying screech. A hundred times more realistic than Harriet's pathetic speaker.

The thump as I heaved it up on to the first step echoed into the high ceiling. Then another thump, and another, as I slowly hauled the extinguisher up the stone staircase. It was getting heavier and I had to pause halfway up to change hands. But all the while I imagined Harriet, hiding in the shadows of the Gallery. Predator turned prey as she stood quaking while the Executioner's axe thumped up each step.

By the time I reached the landing at the top of the stairs, I was sure my plan was working. There was nothing but silence now. Harriet would be hiding, unsure what was happening. Maybe even cowering in fear, too nervous to call out.

I stood to one side of the open doorway, pulled the safety pin from the extinguisher and raised the hose, ready to fire. Now I just had to wait in the shadows. Wait for Harriet to lose her nerve and come and investigate. I'd imagined this a hundred times,

Harriet inching past me and shrieking in terror as water jetted into the back of her head. Terror turning into misery as she turned to see my grinning face.

I must have waited 20 minutes by those doors, all in all. And I spent most of them imagining the look of shock and horror on Harriet's face.

But nothing can last forever. I've never been very patient, even at the best of times. And after 20 minutes standing on that cold floor, I couldn't help myself.

I inched my head around the open door, down low so I wouldn't be seen.

I squinted to look into the length of the Gallery. At first I saw nothing, but then, as my eyes sharpened, the unmistakeable form of Harriet's sleeping bag made me catch my breath. She lay exactly where I'd left her, collapsed on the floor.

I stood frozen, suddenly aware that something wasn't right. I'd expected Harriet to be hiding, but she just lay there – exactly where I'd left her, dimly lit by the glow from her phone where it had fallen face up.

Something was wrong.

I don't know why I didn't run for help, but I didn't. I just stood there, my mouth filling with spit as I fought back a sudden urge to be sick. I stood and waited, utterly unready for what happened next.

First, the heavy curtains rippled apart, as if caught by a breeze. The veins in my arms began to tingle, fizzing with fear. And then a shape emerged from the gloom at the far end of the Gallery. A figure I recognised from Harriet's photograph, covered in a ragged black cloak.

It was tall, faceless, its head hidden beneath a hood. And it seemed to drift towards Harriet's lifeless body. The creature reached forwards with a gloved hand, and for a moment everything slowed. The torn fabric of its cloak hung low as it leaned over her. I looked on in horror as the hand gently stroked the side of Harriet's face.

And then, from behind me, came a new sound.

Metal on stone.

This was no fire extinguisher.

The sharp screech of an axeblade being dragged across stone was unmistakeable.

The creature's head flicked upwards at the sound, and for the first time it … she … looked at me.

I say she because it was a woman's face, at least in parts. The face of a corpse, flesh half-eaten away by time and Heaven knows what creatures that lurk in the soil of a grave.

No, dissolved, said the voice in my brain. *Dissolved in quicklime. The remaining flesh rotting off the bone of her skull.*

I would probably have screamed then, staring into those black, empty eyes. But a thump from the stairs below drove the air from my lungs. And with my brain spinning in my head, I realised there was only one explanation.

The Executioner had reached the bottom step.

My soul drained away with every thump as the greataxe was heaved up those stairs. And as the Executioner climbed, all I could do was stand frozen. Too terrified to look back, unable to take my eyes off the rotting face ahead of me.

The woman's fear was unmistakeable, and she screamed silently – her tongue just a dissolved stump quivering in her open mouth. But whether it was a scream of fear or warning, I'll never know. Because with a final, resounding thump, the Executioner reached the top of the stairs.

I was trapped.

Doomed.

The axe dragged closer, and I flinched at the sound, still unable to look back. The air became cold, like an icy breath on the back of my neck.

And I knew that I had to do something. Anything to get away.

So I did the only thing I could think of.

Spinning and running, I vaulted the railing at the top of the stairs.

I hung there for a few horrible moments, my feet scrabbling to find a ledge to support my weight – painfully aware how far the fall was and how hard the floor below me. I just had to hang on.

I held on long enough to see the Executioner.

He was nothing like I'd imagined. No hood, no mask. He wasn't even wearing black. But the axe was unmistakeable. He dragged it onwards like it weighed a thousand tonnes. The misery of long centuries etched on his face as he walked on into the Gallery.

I tried to climb back over the railing. I really did. But without a foothold, it was hopeless. My grip began to weaken almost immediately, and my hands to slip. And then gravity really got to work – and my body was yanked violently into the void of the stairwell and on to the hard stone floor below.

I can only guess what happened after that. Because the next thing I remember was waking on the floor of the hall. It was dark, and the room was empty, but there was police tape everywhere.

I had a sense that time had passed, and as I sat up and looked around the empty hallway, I somehow knew that I'd passed, too. I'd become yet another ghost of Hampton Court Palace.

***

I no longer feel anything now I'm a ghost. Not warmth nor cold, not hunger, thirst, happiness, joy – nothing. Unlike Catherine, I don't even feel fear, or pain. Not even boredom. I sometimes think I'd like to feel miserable or sad. But I can't even do that.

There's just one thing that drives me to wake each night. And every night it's the same. I go to the corner of the entrance hall and find a fire extinguisher. The big one, marked 'WATER'. And I drag it up those stone stairs, one giant thump at a time. And then, at the entrance to the Gallery, I wait.

Because one day, Harriet might come back. And if she ever does, I'll be waiting. Ready to scare her, quite literally, to death.

AFTERWORD

It was late at night and Hampton Court was in darkness. I was on my way home after a long day at work and decided to take the scenic route, along the so-called 'Haunted Gallery', named after the unquiet spirit of Henry VIII's ill-fated fifth wife, Catherine Howard. There have been more ghostly sightings, experiences and faintings along this single stretch of the palace than anywhere else. However, that was far from my mind as I enjoyed the peace of the usually bustling space, pausing now and then to admire one of the exquisite paintings of the Tudor dynasty.

I had progressed about halfway along when the temperature suddenly dropped. It was as if I had walked into a freezer. I stood stock-still and looked for signs of a draught – an open window or door, perhaps. There were just solid walls. Then, as quickly as it had come, the coldness disappeared and the atmosphere returned to normal. It is the closest I have come to experiencing anything that might be considered paranormal activity during my 17 years of working for Historic Royal Palaces.

As Chief Historian, I keep an open mind about such things. Many of my colleagues have seen or experienced things that can be described as at best unusual and at worst, downright spooky. From 'Skeletor', a man dressed in Tudor clothes who was caught on CCTV flinging open security doors in a part of the palace where no visitors are permitted, to the ghost of Catherine Howard, running screaming along the Haunted Gallery as she tries in vain to reach Henry VIII and plead for her life. My fellow workers are all perfectly rational people, not determined ghost hunters, seizing on a trick of a camera light as an 'orb' and hearing every creak of a floorboard as the tread of a spectral visitor. No, they have usually just been going about their business, just as I was that night, when suddenly they encountered what may have been a presence from another world.

Believer or sceptic, I am fascinated by the

AFTERWORD

many ghost stories associated with our palaces. Researching them can often lead to dead ends (no pun intended), but just occasionally they can uncover previously hidden people and stories. One of my favourites is Sybil Penn, Edward VI's beloved childhood nurse. She went on to serve his sister Elizabeth when she became queen and paid for her unflinching devotion with her life. Elizabeth had only been queen for four years when, in 1562, she was staying at Hampton Court and contracted smallpox, one of the most feared and deadly diseases of the age. Not caring for her own safety, Sybil nursed her royal mistress back to health but sadly caught the disease herself and died within days. She is thought to be the 'Grey Lady' who is regularly seen wandering the courtyards of the palace, as well as wreaking havoc at nearby St Mary's Church, Hampton, where she lies buried.

Behind many of the other ghostly legends at our palaces lie real people who lived, worked and died here. Some, such as Anne Boleyn, Lady Jane Grey and Catherine Howard, lived their lives in the spotlight, enjoying meteoric rises before their untimely, bloody ends. But others were simply part of the palace community, working in the kitchens, sweeping out the fireplaces, carving the emblems of the latest wife of Henry VIII. Perhaps their

Afterword

unquiet spirits really do live on, but even if they don't, I'm grateful to those ghost stories for opening a window into the past and enabling us to discover some of the hidden histories of our palaces.

I hope you've enjoyed this haunting book as much as I have. The stories it contains might be figments of their authors' imaginations, but the fact that they are inspired by real people, events and places from our wonderful palaces earns them pride of place on my bookshelves – and I hope yours, too.

Tracy Borman OBE
Chief Historian, Historic Royal Palaces

INSPIRATION AND BIOGRAPHIES

JIM HELMORE
Click, Clack

Ghostly goings-on in history have always held a special place in my heart, so it was a joy to be able to set this story in the actual Tower of London, the site of so many spine-chilling events. As much has already been said about the Tower's famous prisoners, I wanted my story to feature a few of its less well-known residents, like the everyday workers who kept the place running.

I'm also fascinated by the supernatural idea of 'time-slips', where people believe they've briefly been transported back to different periods in the past. A visit to the Tower today is a bit like experiencing a time-slip: it's easy to imagine the famous events that happened there as so much of the original building remains the same today, but what if we could actually go back and experience that history first-hand?

Animals of one sort or another play a big part in many of my favourite stories, so I decided to base this tale on the Tower's much-loved ravens. Not only are ravens entwined with the Tower's history – a mysterious legend states that if they were ever to leave, 'the Tower and all England would fall' – but they are also a staple ingredient of so many classic ghost stories.

When I visited recently, I met most of the Tower's current ravens, including one of the youngest, Poppy. She was perching by the main gate, treating everyone who passed to a display of click-clack calls and nods. She seemed very friendly and not at all timid or afraid of the crowds. Her stare was curious, intelligent and just a little foreboding. This story is dedicated to her.

Jim Helmore lives in London and has been writing children's books for over 20 years. His work includes the award-winning Stripy Horse series and international picture book hit, *The Snow Lion*, which has now been translated into 21 different languages.

E.L. NORRY
The Prince in the Painting

The inspiration for my story came from the painting of Edward VI in the National Portrait Gallery, which had a big impact on me when I first saw it. Just imagining the weight of responsibility Edward would have been under at such a young age. And then, seeing the painting of him at Hampton Court Palace, I wondered what it would be like if he could see and hear and feel. What it might be like if you were actually him – still alive, but in a sort of 'living coma'? Then, as so often happens with inspiration, my 'What Ifs' led to the magic!

I remembered a story in a girls' annual that I read when I was between nine and eleven. This story terrified me so much that I still shudder now remembering the end, where a mean girl gets trapped in a painting forever.

E.L. Norry writes a wide range of fiction, including historical, fantasy and action-adventure stories. She has also published non-fiction titles, including the biographies of Lionel Messi and Nelson Mandela, and has worked on *Black in Time* with Alison Hammond and *Where Are You Really From?* with Adam Rutherford. She has also written for the BBC soap opera, *EastEnders*.

IMOGEN RUSSELL WILLIAMS
Charlie's Ghost

My inspiration for Charlie's Ghost *first came from the idea of Queen Charlotte's cottage. I loved the thought of it being like a little Wendy house for royalty – a playful refuge from life in the palace spotlight. Oppressed by her darker feelings, 12-year-old Charlie is also in need of refuge and Queen Charlotte's cottage seemed exactly the place where a sad, angry girl might meet her ghostly namesake and have powerful visions of the past.*

Imogen Russell Williams is a children's book critic and author of children's non-fiction, including *Great Britons* and *The Big Book of the UK*, as well as poetry for all ages. She is currently writing her first young adult novel.

FARIDAH ÀBÍKÉ-ÍYÍMÍDÉ
The Haunted Masque

I have always found history really interesting – the idea that someone hundreds and hundreds of years ago might've walked in my exact same footsteps. For the same reason, I have always loved old historical sites like museums, castles and palaces as they serve as tangible evidence to those of us today that there were people who lived before. The historic royal palaces in particular are some of the most unique places in the country. Their history is so well-preserved, you don't have to try too hard to imagine the events that once unfolded there, or the people who once walked those paths.

My story was inspired by one of the darker historical events that took place at Banqueting House – King Charles I's beheading. I started wondering what it might be like for the monarch as a ghost trapped in this beautiful but much-changed place for centuries, and the sort of things that might interest a 17th century king.

Inspiration and Biographies

Faridah Àbíké-Íyímídé is the New York Times and international bestselling and award-winning author of *Ace of Spades*, *Where Sleeping Girls Lie* and other books for young adults.

SAM SEDGMAN
Children of the Maze

I've loved mazes since I was a kid: solving them, drawing them, making them in the garden out of sticks. I actually won a school prize for a special project on the history of mazes. Most summers, I would talk my parents into taking me to visit one of the many hedge mazes in England, so I could get lost in one for real. (My favourite is the one at Longleat Safari Park, the largest in the country, which has bridges).

My mum grew up not too far from Hampton Court, and when we visited the palace, I was fascinated to discover that she still remembered the maze's 'secret'. I loved the idea of a maze that we meet in childhood leaving its mark on us – one that stays in our memories, and perhaps even changes them. When I was asked which historic royal palace might inspire me to write a ghost story, there was no question that I was going to write about the maze at Hampton Court Palace. I thought about what scary things might be lurking at the heart of a maze that a child might have to confront – being abandoned, being forgotten, not understanding the rules of life. I put all that in, and then I added a hedge that eats people. Because, why not?

Sam Sedgman is a bestselling author, confirmed nerd and enthusiastic ferroequinologist (someone who studies trains). Forever interested in piecing things together, he is a lifelong fan of puzzles, games and detective fiction, and once founded a company making murder mystery treasure hunts for adventurous Londoners. His books have been translated into more than 20 languages.

JOSEPH COELHO OBE
A Braid of Seeds

I have always loved gardening and the joy that planting a seed can bring. I am especially interested in heritage seed varieties and the movement to protect seeds for future generations. On discovering the history surrounding seed-saving for survival, as carried out by African slaves during the transatlantic slave trade, I was deeply moved. It is believed they took seeds when they could during their horrendous sea voyage and braided these seeds into their hair, keeping them secure and safe so that should they be able to escape, they would be able to survive.

I found the foresight, bravery and risks taken to do such a thing incredibly inspiring and upsetting. It speaks to me of the human endeavour to survive against the most horrific of conditions – it also speaks to me of the human ability to hope. We know of these acts both from the oral tradition in Suriname amongst communities that are descendants of escaped slaves and from the crops they grow; crops that can be traced back to Africa.

Inspiration and Biographies

King George III regularly received flora samples from botanists such as Sir Joseph Banks. Since the slave trade was still very much alive during his reign, threads of a story began to emerge – one that could explore the lives of enslaved people and how their actions have endured into the present.

Joseph Coelho OBE is a multi-award-winning children's author. His YA novels have received international acclaim and he has written plays for all the top London children's theatres, amongst others. He is two-time winner of the Indie Book Awards Picture Book Category and in 2024 won the Carnegie Medal for *The Boy Lost in the Maze* (illustrated by Kate Milner). Joseph was the Waterstones Children's Laureate from 2022 to 2024.

Alexia Casale
The Sundial

When I was researching Banqueting House, I realised that John Webb (who, aged 17, became live-in assistant to Banqueting House's architect Inigo Jones) would have been 11 or 12 when the building was finished. Since John went on to marry Anne Jones (a relative of Inigo Jones), I loved the idea that the three of them met and had an adventure in 1622. Even though there's no evidence of them meeting, I thought this could have led to the offer of apprenticeship after John finished at Merchant Taylors' School.

A time-slip story let me explore the history of the current Banqueting House and the previous banqueting halls that stood on the site. Then, when I discovered that the old sundial at Whitehall Palace (with the Fowler inscription) was replaced (with one designed by mathematician and astronomer, Edmund Gunter) around the time that Banqueting House was completed, I felt I had the perfect ingredients for a bit of magic.

Dr Alexia Casale is an author of fiction for children, teens and adults, as well as Reader in Writing for Young People at Bath Spa University. She is the co-founder of Literature across Borders – a project to help children's books travel across borders: there is now a schools programme for kids to join in! She also consults on scripts for theatre, film and TV.

SOPHIE KIRTLEY
In This Still Place

One of the most extraordinary things about Hillsborough Castle is its gardens – with its woodlands and waterways, a cave and an ice house, rose bushes and apple trees. It's a landscape of many moods and many stories. When writing my story, what I set out to do most of all was to see the castle and its grounds from a child's perspective. And when I learned that back in the 18th and 19th centuries, pineapples were cultivated here, I knew I had a fantastic piece of real-life context to inspire my story.

Around the time my story is set, pineapples were a real status symbol. Originating in warmer climates, like South America, they were so special and expensive that wealthy pineapple owners didn't even eat them. Instead, they kept them on display to show off to visitors!

But guess what? Northern Ireland is NOT a warm place! So to make the pineapples flourish, a complicated system of hot houses and furnaces was needed. And who would've kept these furnaces flaming through the long winter nights? A young furnace boy, of course.

Leaning into the history of pineapple growing, my story explores Hillsborough Castle and Gardens through different children's eyes. I didn't want to just consider how a wealthy child would have experienced this place, but also the life and experiences of an ordinary working child.

Sophie Kirtley is a prize-winning children's author from Belfast. Her debut novel *The Wild Way Home* was Waterstones Children's Book of the Month and was shortlisted for the Joan Aiken Future Classics Prize. Sophie grew up in Northern Ireland where she spent her childhood exploring secret attics, shadowy forests and crumbling castles. Nowadays she lives in Wiltshire with her husband, three children and perhaps even a ghost or two!

CATHERINE JOHNSON
Run, Rabbit, Run

I lived in East London for more than half of my life and I'd pass the Tower of London sometimes. Seeing a real-life castle that was one of the founding buildings of our city, just there on the Thames, always felt a bit magic. I do honestly think there's a kind of magic in a building like that. A building that's seen so much in its thousand-year history. It's just stuffed full of millions of stories, and not all of them are about the Tudors or the ravens that live there.

I remember hearing plenty of stories about the terrifying times real-life gangsters made many ordinary East Enders' lives miserable. Eddie is living right in the middle of these times. And, although my story is set over ten years after World War Two, shadows of the war are all around Eddie – even for me growing up in the late '60s, there were bomb sites and reminders of what the city, and ordinary Londoners, had gone through. I sort of knitted together the true story of the last man to be executed at the Tower with the story of a boy who has a lot of choices to make.

Catherine Johnson has written more than 25 books for young readers including *Race To The Frozen North* and *Sawbones*, as well as for film, radio and TV. Her next book, *Dance of Resistance*, is a biography of the superstar dancer and spy, Josephine Baker.

Inspiration and Biographies

JASMINE RICHARDS
The Doll's House

My story was inspired by a visit to Kensington Palace, where I encountered a striking doll's house and learnt about the restrictive Kensington System. I combined this with research into Sarah Forbes Bonetta, a young woman from West Africa, who was made a godchild of Queen Victoria when she was seven years old. I also wanted to centre her daughter, Victoria Matilda (Tilly) Davies. In the historical record about Tilly, there is just a single line noting that she learnt of her mother's death whilst on her way to visit Queen Victoria at Osborne House. I couldn't stop thinking about that moment and what might have happened. I wanted to explore how memories and trauma can be passed on not only through people, but also through places and objects.

Jasmine Richards is an award-winning author and the founder and chief storyteller at Storymix, a fiction studio dedicated to inclusive and innovative storytelling. Known for her fantasy-adventure novels, including *The Unmorrow Curse* and *The Myth Keeper*, she is also the co-author of the festive tale for young readers, *The Other Father Christmas*.

Inspiration and Biographies

LARRY HAYES
The Executioner

I've always wanted to be a ghost hunter, ever since visiting Hampton Court Palace as a kid. Our smiling tour guide told us all about the different palace ghosts and then, suddenly, looked very serious. That's when she told us about a ghost she'd seen herself. On her way home, in the dusky evening, she had looked up from the courtyard to see a figure in the window of the Haunted Gallery. She ran, apparently, without even looking back.

From that point on, I vowed to become a real life ghost hunter. I've slept in haunted hotels and houses all over the world and I've seen things I really can't explain. But, you know what? Nothing could be better than a night at Hampton Court Palace. That's why I wrote this story. In the hope that one day, I'll get a 'Royal Invite' to sleep over there, just like Jack and Harriet. So if you ever meet the King, please do mention it.

Larry Hayes is the author of many books for children, including *The Nightmares of Finnegan Quick* and his comedy sci-fi series, How to Survive (which won 'Funniest Book' at the Laugh Out Loud Book Awards). Larry combines writing with helping to manage an award-winning charity for disadvantaged and homeless young people, working in finance and being a governor of a primary school federation.

PAM SMY
Illustrator for *Ghosts in the Walls*

When I was a child, my family lived for a few years in a house that was haunted. It wasn't a terrifying thing like you see in the movies; the extra 'presence' in the house was just part of our everyday lives. After years of working on many different types of books for all ages, I find that I most enjoy illustrating ghost stories ... an echo of my own childhood experience in that cottage.

I now live in a beautiful town with a ruined castle in the middle of it, and the remains of an old abbey in the churchyard. The river that weaves around the town gives rise to wispy mists in the morning. It is the perfect inspiration for imagining all sorts of people from the past living among us today.

Pam Smy has illustrated books for authors such as John Agard, Penelope Lively, Lucy Strange, Julia Green and Linda Newbery, specialising in stories with ghostly and mysterious atmospheres. As an author her first novel, *Thornhill*, was shortlisted for the CILIP Greenaway Award and the Waterstones Prize.

YVETTE FIELDING
Foreword

Yvette Fielding is a television presenter, producer, actress, writer and paranormal investigator. She co-created and presented the Most Haunted series, followed by *Ghosthunting With...* for ITV2, firmly establishing her as 'first lady of the paranormal'. Yvette is also an author, whose work includes the acclaimed children's series The Ghost Hunter Chronicles.

TRACY BORMAN OBE
Afterword

Tracy Borman OBE is a bestselling author, British historian, and broadcaster and is currently Chief Historian for Historic Royal Palaces. She is also Professor and Chancellor of Bishop Grosseteste University, Lincoln, and Chief Executive of the Heritage Education Trust.